CINDERELLA'S
SECRET
ROYAL FLING

CINDERELLA'S SECRET ROYAL FLING

JESSICA GILMORE

MILLS & BOON

First published in Great Britain 2019
by Mills & Boon, an imprint of HarperCollins*Publishers*
1 London Bridge Street, London, SE1 9GF

Large Print edition 2019

© 2019 Jessica Gilmore

ISBN: 978-0-263-08312-5

MIX
Paper from
responsible sources
FSC® C007454

Printed and bound in Great Britain
by CPI Group (UK) Ltd, Croydon, CR0 4YY

'We've had a beautiful friendship,
Diana. We've never marred it by one
quarrel or coolness or unkind word....'
—*Anne of the Island*

To Sam, a true kindred spirit,
thank you for a beautiful friendship.
I've been so lucky to have you
in my life xxx

CHAPTER ONE

The Royal House of Armaria invites you
to a Midsummer Ball
June 21
Time: 7 p.m. until late
Place: Armaria Castle
Dress code: Black tie
RSVP

LAURENT PICKED UP the sample cream and gold heavily embossed card and turned it over. The other side was blank, awaiting a name. Strange to think that in less than a week this card would be one of the hottest tickets in town. No, not just in town, in Europe.

After all, it had been over twenty years since Armaria had hosted one of their famous Midsummer Balls, enough time for the opulent occasions to become part of myth and legend; rumour whispered that anything might happen to those lucky enough to attend. Film stars fell in love with royalty, maids married dukes and unhappy countesses ran away with stable boys. Every Midsummer Ball was filled with wonder, with seduction, with magic.

At least, if you believed the stories they were. The reality was probably a lot more prosaic. After all, if Laurent's plans came to fruition, one day stories might be told about this year's ball, a tale of a midnight proposal and a fairy tale romance. His clasp tightened on the card. Luckily he was too old to believe in fairy tales and he had never dreamt of romance. All a man in his position could do was hope for compatibility and liking.

He turned as the library door opened and his mother entered the book-lined room, relief on her face as she spotted him. Replacing the card onto his desk, he covered it hastily with a blank piece of paper and walked out to meet her in the middle of the vast room.

She held out a regal hand towards him. 'Laurent, I haven't seen you since you returned from England. So this is where you've been hiding yourself.'

'Hardly hiding, Maman,' he protested as he bent to kiss her still unlined cheek. 'My aide knew I was in here. As did the maid who brought me my coffee.' He gestured to the small table set with a coffee service pulled up to one of the sofas dotted around the room. 'It's still hot. May I pour you a cup?'

'Thank you, dear.' The dowager Archduchess took a seat on the antique sofa with her usual unhurried elegance, her feet crossing at the ankle, back ramrod-straight and head tilted. Even when it was just the two of them she didn't allow herself to relax. Her hair was always perfectly styled, her make-up fresh, her clothes smart. The message had been drilled into him since he was a small boy; as a member of the Armarian ruling family—the most prominent and important member—he was always on display, always representing his country, and even when alone he could not, must not, forget it.

Pouring his mother a cup of the fragrant coffee, Laurent handed it to her and she accepted it with a gracious nod of thanks. 'Thank you, Laurent. But you must know, it's no time to be hiding in the library. The Prime Minister has been looking for you. He's hoping for an answer…'

'No, he's hoping for a different answer. And he won't get one.' With practised effort Laurent kept the anger out of his voice. 'I will not allow him to turn Armaria into some kind of grubby little tax haven. My grandfather and father managed without taking that step; you managed without taking that step. I won't be the one to sell the country out. Our people deserve better.'

'Our people deserve new roads and houses, better hospitals, more schools…'

'Which is why we need a long-term strategy.' It was as if they were two actors rehearsing well known lines. Lines they had been repeating for the three years since Laurent had finished his MBA and his mother had formally ceded her regency of Armaria to him.

'And you have one?' Hope brightened her voice. 'How was your trip to England? Did he say yes?'

She didn't need to specify who *he* was; she knew full well that Laurent had been paying a second under-the-radar visit to Mike Clayton, the tech entrepreneur whose robotic gadgets could be found in households all over the globe. Mike Clayton who was looking for a more sustainable form of energy to manufacture said robots. Energy a small country with a long coastline, windswept hills and mountains and long hours of sunshine could provide...

Laurent walked over to the tall thin windows, staring out at the famous castle gardens full of tourists and sightseers. Tourism was a valuable resource for the small country, but it wasn't enough to make it as prosperous as it needed to be. 'Not exactly. But he didn't say no either and he's coming out to take a second look at the proposed site and to meet with the university.'

'That's promising. But is it enough? I know the Prime Minister is hoping to have a plan approved by Parliament before the summer break. You need something more concrete than a second visit to offer him.'

'I need nothing. Parliament is merely advisory and the Prime Minister would do very well to remember that.' Laurent inhaled slowly as he turned to face his mother. 'You know that my father was determined not to go down the tax haven route, nor did he want to turn the country into a giant theme park of romanticism and cod medievalism. You worked hard to keep his vision alive and I won't betray his legacy. If we can attract one thriving tech company like Clay Industries then others will be sure to follow. We can turn Armaria into the tech capital of Europe, a Silicon Valley of the north. Create jobs and prosperity without losing our integrity.' He stopped abruptly, aware he sounded like he was giving a prepared speech to Parliament, and his mother smiled with understanding. After all, she had heard variations on the speech many times before.

'It's not me you have to convince, Laurent.'

'No, just Parliament.' Advisory they might be, but life was infinitely easier with them on side. 'If Clay Industries bite then Parliament will capitulate on the tax haven bill, I know it. I just need that first investment…'

'So you'll find a way to make it happen.' His mother was matter-of-fact. This was what they did. Through ten centuries the Archdukes of Armaria had done whatever they had to, to protect their people from invaders and plagues, wars and famine, bankruptcy and poverty. He would not be the first to fail.

'Yes. I will. Which is why I have suggested that the Claytons are our guests of honour for the newly revived Midsummer Ball. Mike Clayton's sixtieth birthday falls on the same day, and they have yet to decide on the best way to mark it. What better way than for him to celebrate here in Armaria on one of the most iconic nights of the year?'

'Midsummer is always special, but it's less than a month away. And it's been years since we held a grand ball. Not since your father...' Her voice faltered, as it still did whenever she spoke of her late husband. Twenty-one years of widowhood hadn't lessened her grief. Things might have been different if she had been able to move on, but instead Laurent was all too aware that his mother's life had stilled at the moment of her husband's death and she had been trapped into a regency she had neither asked for nor wanted, preserving the small country to hand on to her son. 'There is so much to do, to plan and arrange. The ballroom could do with a lick of paint and a polish, as could half that wing and some of our staterooms.'

'It's a good thing we have a castle full of staff, isn't it? I know the timing is tight, Maman, but our Midsummer Balls were legendary; reviving them is the kind of gesture we need to show we have faith in Armaria, in our past and traditions as well as in our future. It's the ideal opportunity to make the Claytons fall in love with Armaria, with everything we have to offer. Let Mike Clayton use his heart as well as his head when he chooses us. Speaking of which…' He hesitated. Once he'd said the next words, there would be no going back. He steeled himself. 'I think it's time I got married.'

'Married?' His mother's surprise was almost comical. After all, she had been hinting at this very thing for two years now, drawing up lists of eligible and connected young ladies on a regular basis.

'I *am* twenty-eight, as you keep reminding me. And, as you know, Alex is next in line—how cross would he be if I died without an heir and he had to become Archduke?'

'Dear Alex,' his mother murmured. 'He loves that hospital so much.'

'Which is why I need to settle down and have an heir or two so he doesn't have to worry about hanging up his stethoscope and putting on a crown.'

The dowager Archduchess's eyes narrowed as she assessed her son. 'I didn't know you were seeing anyone.' And, her tone implied, if she didn't know about it, then how could it be happening? 'And you know how it is. You *are* Armaria and you have to do what is right for the whole country, and that includes your marriage. You can't just marry anyone.'

'I wasn't planning on marrying just anyone.' He took a deep breath. Once the words were said there was no going back. 'Mike Clayton has a daughter. Bella. I'm sure you'll like her. I am considering asking her to be my Archduchess. To strengthen the ties between Armaria and Clay Industries on every level.'

'I see.' His mother blinked and for one moment the formidable regent disappeared, to be replaced with a tearful mother who only wanted her son's happiness. Another blink and the regent returned as if she had never left. 'Oh, Laurent. I do see. And of course it makes sense. The days when we needed to ally ourselves with one of our neighbours through marriage may have gone, but there's always a new generation of buccaneers in town.'

'I haven't said anything to Bella or her parents,' Laurent warned his mother. 'I wanted to discuss it with you first. Obviously, she might have plans for her life that don't include a draughty old castle and living in a strange country.'

'Tell me about her. What makes her laugh? What are her dreams?'

Laurent shifted from one foot to another, uncomfortable with the whimsical question. He was an Archduke. He didn't deal with dreams and laughter; he dealt with facts and figures and if he decided to propose to Bella Clayton and if she accepted then it would be the oldest trade in the book. He had a country in need of investment and her family had that investment to make. A title and a throne for money or influence or protection, just as his forebears had done time and time again.

'As you know, I've stayed with her family twice now and she seems nice enough.' He didn't need to see his mother wince to realise how far short those words fell. 'She's pretty, possibly even beautiful,' he tried again. 'She loves dogs and horses; we spent most of our time together discussing them.' A mutual love of animals was surely as good a place to start a marriage as any. Many royal couples had less.

'Where was she educated?'

'Nothing to worry about there; she went to an exclusive boarding school and then spent a couple of years at a Swiss finishing school. Since then she has worked for Clay Industries, helping run their charity trust.' Not that she seemed over-burdened with a nine-to-five; her role there seemed more titular, but the charity angle would go down well with the press and was good preparation for many of the duties necessary for an Archduchess.

His mother raised an eyebrow. 'No university? That's a shame. I do think in these uncertain times a girl needs a good education beyond correct knives and the right curtsey—she never knows when she might end up Regent in an absolute monarchy. A good grasp of mathematics and economics can be essential.'

A wave of sympathy swept over Laurent for the young Archduchess his mother had once been, barely thirty, widowed and thrust into a position of responsibility on behalf of her young son. 'Hopefully, it won't come to that. I'm not planning on leaving her to manage alone.'

She glanced up, startled, betrayed into an answering smile when she realised he was teasing her. 'Of course not. But an Archduchess does need a lot of common sense and a thick skin as well as brains. It's not an easy job.'

'No. It's not. But she does seem fully aware of the burdens of her privilege as well as the blessings. And her mother made sure I knew that Bella is descended from the Normans on both sides of her family tree—Mike Clayton informally adopted her when he married her mother, but her natural father was a baron, so her background is good enough for those people who care about such things.'

'Yes, it does sound as if her birth and education will do. Laurent, is this idea yours, or have her parents hinted that the two of you might make a suitable union?'

'All my idea. There has been no pressure from Mike Clayton, no hints that his investment is conditional on such a move. But he is extremely fond of his stepdaughter and very family-orientated. I believe he would welcome our marriage and would want to do his best for the place she eventually calls home.' Bella's mother, Simone, was a different story; she had made several comments linking Laurent and her daughter during his two visits to the family estate and taken every opportunity to throw them together. Laurent had no doubt that she was hoping for exactly this outcome—and that with a proposal would come her complete backing for Clay Industries' investment in Armaria.

'And the young lady herself. Does she seem to like you, Laurent? Will she welcome a proposal after so short an acquaintance? Can you be happy with her?'

They were three very different questions.

'I will be happy watching Armaria prosper,' he said at last. 'As for Bella Clayton... I do not believe a proposal will be either a surprise, or unwelcome. She's twenty-seven and has been raised with an expectation of a place in society. Life here would not be the kind of shock it might be for someone from a different kind of background.'

'Well, then,' his mother said after a pause. 'In that case I look forward to meeting her—and her family. When are you hoping that they will arrive?'

'A few days before the ball.' Walking over to the desk, he unearthed the invitation he had been looking at earlier and handed it to his mother. 'I had this mocked up earlier. Once we're happy with the design we'll get them sent out, so get your secretary to send mine the list of everyone you would like to invite by the end of the week. I know the timing is tight, but this is the first royal ball held at the castle for two decades. I don't think any guests will worry too much about prior plans, do you? And, hopefully, by the end of the summer Armaria will have both new investment and a new Archduchess.'

His mother looked around the library, lips pursed. 'I'll also make a list of all the work that needs doing between now and then. It will have to be all hands on deck if we are going to open the castle up to hundreds of guests.'

'I'm happy to wield a paintbrush if it gets the job done. Thank you. Don't worry about the ball itself, Maman. Simone Clayton has recommended an events planner and, all being well, she should be starting at the weekend.' He hesitated. 'Obviously, I expect to cover all costs, as the host, but the Claytons do have some additions they'd like to make to the traditional plans—and of course they have their own list of guests to invite. As a result, they are insisting on paying for the event planner, their guests and for the cost of any of their extra requirements. I did my best to dissuade them, as you can imagine, but they were adamant.' Laurent's mouth thinned. His country, his castle, his responsibility. But he was supposed to be wooing Mike Clayton—and his daughter—not arguing with them, and in the end gracious capitulation was the only option.

'I see. Are you sure, Laurent? Sure that this girl will make you happy?'

Laurent merely bowed in answer. 'I know exactly what I'm doing, both for myself and for Armaria.'

For Laurent knew there was no real difference. He was the Archduke and with the title came responsibility for every man, woman and child, every meadow and mountain. He had never wasted any time wishing things were different; what was the point? His focus had to be on the future—and now his plans were finally coming to fruition. What was the point of might-have-beens and if-onlys? Bella Clayton was attractive, pleasant, well brought up and well connected—and the heir to a company with the capacity to change

Armaria's fortunes. If she was prepared to grant him those assets in return for a title then he was a fortunate man indeed.

Emilia Clayton leaned back in her chair and managed to summon up a professional almost-smile as she regarded her stepmother across the vintage desk.

'You didn't have to make an appointment to see me, Simone.' Only both women knew that was a lie. Emilia did everything she could to avoid her father's family. She was sure they were as relieved as she was when she excused herself from dinners and birthdays. Which was why Simone's presence in her office was such a surprise, and not one of the pleasant variety. Just the sight of her stepmother made it hard for Emilia to be the quiet, controlled professional woman she had grown into, the memory of the rebellious teen with more anger than she could control shuddering through every nerve and vein. She shoved the memories back and maintained her smile.

Simone's almost-smile was as faux genuine as Emilia's own. 'You didn't reply to your father's last texts. An official appointment seemed like the only way to actually guarantee getting hold of you.'

'If I'd known it was so urgent I would have made the time. But I've been busy. As you can see.' Emilia kept her tone light but something in her chest twisted as she spoke. Was her father ill? His texts had been so noncommittal, the usual wishy-washy hopes that she was well and that he would see her at some unspecified point soon. The same messages he'd been sending her for the last decade—when he remembered. Nondescript, impersonal, a salve to his conscience.

Probably exactly what she deserved.

'I'd heard you started your own business. This is all very quaint.' Her stepmother looked around the spacious office space, with its soothing tones of white and grey and vibrant pictures and soft furnishings, with an air that strongly hinted that quaint was the most neutral word she could come up with.

'I have to say, Emilia, I was very surprised to hear that *you* were living in Chelsea.' The slight emphasis on 'you' conveyed myriad meanings, each one suggesting that Emilia was not the kind of person who belonged in the once bohemian, now rarefied borough.

'No one was more surprised than me, but this is where our agency is based.' The truth was, Chelsea was the last place Emilia would have chosen if she had had a choice. She hadn't ventured to this part of West London since finally leaving home for good at just sixteen; it was far too close to her father's Kensington apartment and there were unwelcome memories around every corner. But when her colleague and friend, Alexandra, had inherited an old townhouse in a beautiful tree-lined street in the heart of the old Chelsea village, it had been the catalyst for the two of them, along with their friends Amber and Harriet, to quit their day jobs and leave their rented rooms in far flung parts of London for the heart of West London.

'Yes, the Happy Ever After Agency. How whimsical.'

'We guarantee happy clients. Speaking of which, is this a business appointment, Simone, or did you just want to catch up? Only we are rather busy.'

Simone raised one eyebrow ever so slightly, her only comment on Emilia's manners. Emilia had never been able to rile her stepmother, no matter how hard she tried. And she had tried. Truth was, Simone had never cared enough about her for her behaviour to really matter, each act of bad behaviour and rudeness an inconvenience rather than a shock. 'Lady Jane Winspear was highly complimentary about the party you organised for her.'

Emilia kept the half-smile in place to hide her confusion. The party in question had been for a pair of particularly spoiled twins. In her opinion, Bella, her stepsister, was equally spoiled but somewhat past the age of unicorn rides and carousels. 'That's good to hear.'

'So when I needed an event planner with immediate effect, I of course thought of you. My way of helping out your little enterprise. I know you're too proud to accept help but I hope you wouldn't be silly enough to turn down paying work.'

Emilia curled her hands into fists under the desk. She had made it clear years ago that she neither wanted or needed anything from her father or his new family. But, although the Happy Ever After Agency was doing well, turning down work would be a foolish move, especially from people as well connected as her father and stepmother. '*You* want to *hire* me?'

'That's why I am here. I would like you to organise your father's sixtieth birthday ball.'

'My father's...' Emilia swallowed. Of course she was aware that her father's sixtieth was less than a month away. How could she not be when his fiftieth had been the occasion when she had packed her bags and walked out of his family and his life, vowing that this time it was for ever? She had planned to spend his sixtieth as she had every one of his birthdays since then: in denial.

'As I said, we're very busy and it's very short notice. And I can't afford any free-bies; this is a new business.' She stopped, slightly appalled by herself as the excuses spilled from her mouth. How did Simone always have this effect on her? It was as if she expected the worst from Emilia and Emilia simply had to oblige her. And the only loser was Emilia herself.

'I'm aware of the short notice. The truth is your father was planning a quiet family birthday.' A family birthday which obviously didn't include Emilia. And that might be partly her choice but it still stung. 'However, he's been invited to be guest of honour at the first Armarian Midsummer Ball to be held in over twenty years.'

This was obviously very impressive news indeed and Emilia did her best to look awed whilst trying to work out where Armaria was. Was it the small country between France and Italy or the small country between Switzerland and Italy? Or was it in the Balkans? 'Congratulations to Dad,' she said and Simone threw her a hard glance.

'Finally your father is getting the recognition he deserves. Of course he will want his friends, family and business partners to attend the ball, and so I offered to supply an event planner to make sure every detail is just how he likes it.' Simone steepled her hands and looked at Emilia, her grey-eyed gaze as hard and piercing as it usually was where her stepdaughter was involved. 'Will you be able to find the time to organise the event of the year or will I need to find another planner? One who *isn't* too busy to accommodate me?'

Emilia's mind whirled as thoughts of palaces and royalty and all the delicious publicity such a job would generate passed swiftly through her mind. How could she turn an opportunity like this down? 'Why me?' she asked bluntly.

Simone's mouth thinned. 'Believe me, Emilia, I thought long and hard about com-

ing here today. I want this ball to be perfect and I haven't forgotten your behaviour
at your father's fiftieth—and nor has he. But
your reputation as an event planner is very
good and I can't believe you'd endanger it
because of some long-held teen angst. And,
whether you like it or not, you know your father better than any stranger ever could. If
you put your mind to it then you can make
sure this ball is as special as he is.'

Emilia's fists tightened. 'I see.'

'There's a lot riding on the evening. Not
only is it your father's birthday but he is considering moving his European headquarters
and new factory to Armaria. We have got to
know the Archduke very well over the last
few months and he and Bella... Well, I don't
want to say too much but I have hopes of a
much, much closer tie with the royal family.
Nothing can go wrong. Is that clear?'

'Crystal.'

'So, you'll do it?'

No. Both Emilia's head and heart spoke
in unison. Emilia might be twenty-six now,

all grown up with her own business and a family of friends she'd assembled herself, but where her father was concerned she was still a hurt, lonely child. And when it came to Simone she was a hurt, angry child. She kept an emotional and a physical distance from them for a reason; she didn't like who she had been when she lived with them, the way she had acted, her desperate bids for attention, each one more extreme than the one before, how out of control she had been. Better to stay far away. It was self-preservation and it had worked over the last few years.

But the event promised to be lucrative and generate a lot of publicity. This wasn't just about her; there were four of them with a lot invested in the future of the agency. She couldn't make a decision like this on her own.

'I need to talk to my partners. The notice is short and there is a lot to do; I'll have to leave for Armaria straight away and that means more work for everyone here. Look, I'll let you know in the morning. Send me numbers and a rough outline of what you need tonight and if they agree then I'll send through a quote first thing.'

'There's no need for a quote. I'll pay whatever you charge.' Simone got to her feet in one elegant movement. 'My assistant will email through the guest list and let you know your contact at the palace. Remember, I expect you to be professional, Emilia. Do not embarrass your father or yourself. No, don't get up. I can see myself out. I'll see you in three weeks. I'm expecting perfection. Do not let me down.'

CHAPTER TWO

'WELL, OF COURSE we'll say no.' Amber's green eyes burned with indignation as she paced up and down the small sitting and dining room housed in a conservatory at the back of the house. The whole of the ground floor was given over to office space apart from the galley kitchen and this light, if slightly cramped, area. Upstairs, the first floor and attic floor each housed two bedrooms and a bathroom; Alexandra and Emilia had one floor, Amber and Harriet the other.

Emilia wasn't sure what lucky star had been shining down on her the Christmas Eve she had decided to stay late at work rather than face her lonely rented room and ready meal for one. As she had finally left the modern South Bank building where she worked she had met first Harriet, then Alexandra and Amber, all, like her, in their early twenties and all with nowhere to go that Christmas. An impromptu drink had lengthened into a meal and, several years later, they were business partners, housemates and sisters, a bond even Harriet's recent engagement to their former boss, Deangelo Santos, couldn't break. Although Harriet officially now lived in Deangelo's penthouse apartment while she and her fiancé looked for the perfect home, she still had her own room at the Chelsea townhouse and often stayed over when Deangelo was out of town. And not even a billionaire fiancé could tempt her to stop working. The Happy Ever After Agency was born of their hopes and dreams. It was far more than a job. Making it work was their top priority and, although they all knew that Deangelo would gladly bankroll them, their independence was too important to allow them to accept a penny.

'Simone will pay whatever I quote, money no object. And think of the publicity, Amber.'

Alex nodded. 'The Archduke of Armaria

is notoriously private. A ball hosted by him, the first in the royal castle in twenty years, will be headlines in all the gossip magazines, headlines which will give us the kind of boost we need to really get ourselves ahead.'

'We're doing okay and we can get ahead another way. Amber's right. You can't be an employee at your own father's birthday.' Harriet squeezed her hand. 'You should be there, dancing the night away, not worrying about missing musicians and whether there's enough canapés.'

'We all know the only way I'll be there is if I can invoice for the privilege. Family gatherings are not my style and it's easier for them to play happy, perfect families without me lurking in the background like the Ghost of Family Past. Look, if we consider this objectively then you know I would be mad to turn it down. It's a great job.' Part of her even believed what she was saying, another part, the bewildered little girl she tried hard to forget, just wanted to be at her dad's birthday party. And the sensible part of her agreed with her friends. She would be much better off turning the event down.

But no way was she giving Simone the satisfaction.

'Do you want any of us there as backup?' Alexandra asked in her usual calm, cool way and Emilia seized onto the practical question gratefully.

'No, thanks. There is plenty to do here; in fact I have another two birthday parties for the pampered Princelings and Princesses of Chelsea, a Golden Wedding and an engagement party in the next three weeks, plus a restaurant launch and a charity coffee morning. Amber, I know you have a lot of your own work on; will you be able to manage?'

'With your notes and if you're on the end of the phone, of course,' Amber said stoutly.

Emilia smiled at her gratefully. 'We always planned to be doing huge charity balls and corporate launches; it's time we moved on from children's games, even if Pass the Parcel has a real diamond bracelet inside. How nice if we got to employ someone to take care of the small events and I could concentrate on the big league. Look, Simone thinks she's putting me down with this whole scheme, but she's actually doing us a huge favour so let's treat this like any other job. Who knows anything about Armaria?'

'Isn't it the smallest country in Europe?' Amber asked, but Harriet shook her head.

'Third, I think, or fourth. It's a principality, but the ruling Prince is actually an Archduke for various historical reasons I can't remember. Armaria is fiercely independent and proud, very patriotic, very beautiful. It's in the sweet spot between France, Switzerland and Italy so gorgeous coastline, mountains and forests. Castles to die for; you couldn't ask for a more picturesque location, Emilia.'

'And how do you know so much about Armaria?' Alex arched elegant eyebrows at her friend.

'Deangelo considered investing there. The Archduke wants industry beyond tourism and farming without going down the tax haven route; it wasn't right for him then but he's been keeping an eye on the place to see how things change. The Archduke's father died when he was just a little boy and his mother was regent for many years and she concentrated on stability not growth, which means the economy has stagnated. It's still an absolute monarchy; there's some agitating for more democracy, but the last referendum was pretty decisive in favour of the status quo.'

Harriet clearly hadn't finished but she was interrupted by a squawk from Amber, who waved her phone in the air. 'According to Your Royal Gossip the pressure is on the Archduke to marry. The next closest heir is an older, unmarried second cousin who runs the local hospital and has no interest in changing that. Rumour is that Prince Laurent d'Armaria is looking outside the usual pool of local aristocrats and European royalty for fresh blood and fresh money...'

'Your stepsister is single, isn't she?' Harriet asked and Emilia nodded.

'As far as I know. Simone was hoping for

a duke or one of the Windsors but obviously that didn't happen. I wonder if that's what she meant by closer ties? What's he like, the Archduke?'

'Handsome in a cold, blond way. Said to be proud, standoffish.' Amber held her phone out to Emilia but she waved it away. She'd see him for herself soon enough.

'Okay, I think we've decided that we're going for it, right? In that case I declare this meeting officially over. Let's celebrate our new contract the usual way.'

'Pyjamas, cheese on toast and mugs of hot chocolate?' Harriet punched the air. 'Bags me choose the film; Deangelo is on a nature documentary phase and it's interesting but I am gasping for a good old-fashioned romcom.'

They all smiled in agreement, but Emilia knew her friends' smiles all masked concern and that they would be watching her carefully all evening long to make sure she was okay. But as she watched Harriet start to slice the sourdough bread she'd brought over from Borough Market, and Amber grate the cheese while Alexandra began to heat the milk, Emilia also knew that she'd survive. She had before, and this time, thanks to the Agency and the girls who ran it, she wasn't on her own.

Emilia was doubly glad of the optimism and support of her friends when, two days later, she found herself suspended over the famous Armarian royal castle. The helicopter engine was so loud she could barely form a sentence, even in her head, but if she could she was sure that sentence would be *Help*. Human beings were not meant to travel in tiny metal cages held up in the air only by rotating rods.

The helicopter hovered over the castle for a brief moment, giving Emilia a bird's-eye view of the ancient building, all delicate spires and battlements, looking more like a child's dream of a castle than a real-life building, home to the royal family of Armaria, seat of the small country's Parliament and famous tourist attraction. Thanks to Harriet's detailed briefings and Simone's even more detailed notes, she knew that the Archdukes of Armaria had lived right here, in this very spot, for generations beyond memory, the original keep long since enfolded into the growing castle, the whole remodelled in the eighteenth century by an Archduke whose tastes had run to the gothic. The sun shone overhead and to one side the sea sparkled a deep blue, to the other the mountains rose up to meet the sky, the very furthest still topped with white. Even through her fear Emilia noted that she had never seen anything more idyllic in her entire life.

She sucked in a deep breath as the helicopter began to descend. She was here; there was no changing her mind now. And she didn't know what was more terrifying: putting together an event for hundreds of people, an event that would be reported on by every gossip magazine and blog in the western world, in just three weeks—or facing her father and his family.

With a final sickening lurch the helicopter juddered to a stop and Emilia gingerly undid her seat belt and alighted, head bent as far down as she could get it even though the blades were far above her. Glad she had elected to wear sensible flats and trousers to travel, she pulled her light linen jacket down and smoothed her hair back, checking it was still in its smooth ponytail. She was here to work and she needed to make the right impression straight off. This she could do. She'd been working since she was sixteen years old and that was the way she liked it. She'd soon learned that the busier she was, the less time she had to think. Or to feel.

A tall, angular woman was waiting at the far end of the helipad and, after seeing that her bags were being collected by a young, uniformed man, Emilia made her way over to her. 'Hi,' she said, holding out her hand in greeting. 'I'm Emilia, the event planner.' It was only as she spoke that she realised she had omitted her surname. Clayton was common enough a name but it might be easier not to be associated with the guest of honour or asked any difficult questions. Emilia only it would be then, unless anyone asked outright.

Her hand was ignored in favour of a condescending nod. 'Come with me. I'll show you to your office. You do not have much time so I hope you are ready to start straight away.'

'That's okay. I once organised a takeover announcement and launch of a whole new brand in just forty-eight hours. I thrive on pressure.' Uncomfortably aware she was beginning to sound over eager and might break out into the crazy metaphors of a reality show contestant any second, Emilia hurriedly changed the subject. 'It's very beautiful here; what an amazing setting. I usually like to start off by walking around a venue, getting to know it properly. Will there be any issue here if I do the same? I'm aware that the building has several functions and that the royal family actually live here and the castle is home to Parliament as well.'

'Your security clearance has been arranged.' As the older lady spoke they arrived at a small side door, guarded by a perspiring man in an antiquated-looking uniform, all braid and gilt. 'This is the door you will use to enter and exit the palace at all times. You need to show your pass here and then sign in once inside. No pass, no admittance, no exception.'

'Understood.' Emilia smiled at the guard, who stared woodenly back before she followed her guide into the long entrance hallway. It took a few moments for her details to be registered, her passport scrutinised and the all-important pass to be issued and she was then led down the corridor, rooms pointed out as they went.

'That's the main aides' office, the housekeeper's room and the *garde de campe*'s suite. You'll find the kitchens along there, turn right and down the stairs; the staff dining room is next to it. Breakfast is available between six and eight, lunch between noon and two and dinner from eight. If you require anything in the meantime, ask a page and she or he will get it for you. You do not help yourself. Most people are fluent in English; the official language is French, but day-to-day we speak an Armarian dialect which is a mixture of Italian and French.'

'I have passable Italian and my mother was French so I should be fine,' Emilia reassured her and the confidence elicited a begrudging smile. This lady was a difficult audience, but she'd had worse.

'Your pass gives you access to everywhere you should need to go. If it's locked then it's a private area, accessible only to the royal family and their immediate staff. You are not to trespass. This side of the castle is the administrative and housekeeping wing and so the royal family are very unlikely to be seen back here, nor should you encounter any Members of Parliament; their offices and debating chambers are on the other side of the castle. If you should see the Archduke or his mother you curtsey and do not speak until spoken to. If you need to check anything with them, you ask me and I will arrange it.'

'Great. And you are?'

The thin lips pursed even tighter. 'Contessa Sophy D'Arbe. The Archduchess's secretary.'

'Got it.' Emilia looked around her with interest. Although the windows were narrow and glazed with ancient-looking glass, the curved ceilings high and the stone underfoot uneven, grey and very old, the corridors were still impersonal and corporate, with nondescript watercolours on the walls and the painted, closed doors were numbered like in any work space.

'Your office is on the floor below; it's small and a little dark, but it was the only space we had available. It should have everything you need, including lists of all the palace suppliers. Your bedroom is in the attic. The key to your room and directions to all areas of the castle are on your desk and your belongings have already been taken to your room.' The Contessa came to a stop by a narrow staircase and nodded to it. 'Your security pass will unlock your office door. Down those stairs, turn right, room twelve. If you need any refreshments, ask a page. I'll arrange a meeting with you tomorrow to see how you've got on. Oh, and welcome to Armaria.' And with that the Contessa nodded one more time before sweeping away without a backward glance.

Emilia stood at the top of the stairs, torn between an urge to laugh and an urge to turn around and scamper back to the safety of her Chelsea home as fast as she could. 'The Contessa and Simone seem destined to become BFFs,' she muttered. 'I must introduce them.' *Right.* She took a deep breath. Time to find and check out the adequate office. Time to locate a page and order some much-needed coffee. Time to write out her first of what would be many to-do lists. And then time to familiarise herself with the castle and the grounds. She had all this wonderful, old, picturesque space to play with. The more she had to do, the less time she had to worry about actually seeing her father. It was time to get busy.

* * *

'Ah, Your Highness…'

'His Royal Highness will know the answer…'

Eyes forward, head up, Laurent silently repeated as he swept down the grand corridor, determinedly not looking left, right or up onto the gallery, where at least three people were trying to grab his attention. He slid his gaze slightly to the right to ensure his Armarian Spaniel, Pomme, was following him, then snapped them straight ahead, allowing one hand to briefly rest on the dog's head as he marched on.

It came to something when a man couldn't find any peace in his own castle. Laurent just wanted a corner to sit and read through the proposal his Chancellor had pressed upon him earlier that day, but every corner seemed to be full of cleaners or decorators or florists. There wasn't an inch of the palace that wasn't being buffed, polished, repainted or reupholstered and the air was thick with paint, dust and turpentine. Even his own suite of rooms wasn't immune, although he had made it very clear to anyone who would listen that they at least were strictly off-limits to cameras, guests and onlookers. Even a prince needed a room of his own—or, in his case, five rooms including a study and a bathroom, his bedroom, dressing room and en suite bathroom, neatly housed in one of the four turrets which rounded off every wing of the castle. Although he would never admit it, Laurent was still secretly glad that he had his own turret room. It seemed like the least a boy growing up in a castle could expect, a small consolation against the lack of privacy and tourists around every corner. Against the role he had no choice but to occupy.

'Just the man! Your Highness...'

But Laurent had long since learned the key to getting from A to B undisturbed. He simply strode fast, head high, eyes not focusing on a single face, not catching anyone's gaze. And because it was considered bad manners—if not downright treasonous—

to accost the Archduke without an explicit invitation, this tactic usually worked. But it was hard to walk purposefully when one had to keep dodging ladders, buckets and toolboxes and every now and then Laurent would accidentally catch someone's eye and that would be considered the explicit permission that person needed to unburden themselves to their sovereign, as was their right and his duty. But when all they wanted was his view on paint colours or a ticket to this damn ball and he had a proposal to read, his patience was wearing thin fast. It was with a huge sense of relief that he finally reached the tiny side door to which only he owned a key and stepped out into the sunny courtyard beyond, the precious proposal a little more bent and dog-eared and still unread. He closed the door firmly behind him as Pomme made a dash for the nearest potted plant.

Laurent tightened his grip on the report. This was his chance: his chance to make Armaria truly independent and stable. Industry, jobs, investment… The Chancellor had gathered all the evidence, ready for Laurent to place it directly in Mike Clayton's hands. He just needed to pick when to present it. Before the ball or after? Before he proposed to Mike Clayton's beloved daughter or after...?

He'd always known he'd have to marry strategically; every Archduke did. Their title and position bartered carefully away for influence or money or hopefully both. Why should he be different just because some modern foreign princes and princesses had been allowed to follow their hearts? In a country where the monarch was more than a figurehead, hearts simply couldn't rule over heads. He'd always known this.

And now the time had come. Proposing to Bella Clayton was the most sensible thing he could do. He'd be fulfilling his duty to the country and to the throne. She was well-bred, well-educated and brought with her the potential of a new beginning for Armaria. She was perfect.

Whistling for Pomme to join him, Laurent walked across the shady courtyard, filled with tall plants in earthenware pots and brightly flowering climbing plants. An arched door led into a walled garden, half a flower-filled lawn, half a small tangled orchard of fruit trees. At the far end of the orchard, a small wrought iron arbour stood by the wall, a shady respite from the relentless noon sun, and Laurent's favourite hiding place. Checking his phone—only eight missed calls, fifteen messages and thirty-three emails since he'd last looked half an hour ago—he headed straight there while Pomme, ecstatic to be freed from palace etiquette, made for the nearest tree. Laurent absentmindedly scrolled through the emails, deleting or forwarding as many as he could, flagging the rest to deal with later.

Intent on his phone, he didn't notice a leg lying in his path, not until he tripped right over it, recalled to his surroundings by an indignant, 'Ouch! Watch where you're going!'

Regaining his balance, Laurent turned and looked down at a young, slim woman, lying under a tree, long legs sticking out in a most dangerous way. 'I shouldn't need to watch where I'm going,' he said in his most repressive manner. 'This garden is private.'

It was only as he spoke that he realised the young woman had spoken and he had replied in English.

Flushing to the roots of her honey-brown hair, the young woman immediately scrambled to her feet, notebook in one hand, pen in the other. 'I did wonder,' she confessed. 'The door was so well concealed, but when it opened...'

'You slipped inside and hoped no one would see you?' It should have been locked. Only two gardeners had the key; one of them had slipped up.

'That's about the truth of it. They gave me an office, but it's so noisy in the palace I couldn't think so I rewarded myself for a solid afternoon's work with an explore of the gardens. I couldn't believe my luck when I found this place. Not that the rest of the gardens aren't exquisite,' she added hurriedly. 'But they are so formal. I like a bit of wildness in my nature. I'm Emilia—' she stuck the pen into a pocket and held out a hand '—the event organiser. I am so sorry. I promise not to trespass again.'

Laurent was slow to take her hand, struck as he was by two things. One was the frank expression in her clear hazel eyes, an expression untinged by awe. The other was her surprising admission that she preferred this small, shady garden to the famous royal gardens of Armaria. He did, of course, but as far as he knew he was in a minority of one. 'You don't like the Royal Gardens?'

She stepped back, hand dropping as she looked around at the orchard as if seriously considering his question. 'Oh, no, they are beautiful and they will make a wonderful backdrop for the ball. But they're very...' she paused '...very grand. And perfect. I worry about crushing a blade of grass, or casting a shadow on a carefully cultivated scene. I'm much more of a throw myself on the ground and sprawl kind of girl, as you found out. Sorry again.'

'In that case,' Laurent said, 'you must come here whenever you wish. I'll order you a key.'

'But this is obviously private; won't the Archduke mind?'

For a moment all Laurent could do was stand there with an expression he was sure was the most undignified one he'd worn since ascending to the Dukedom at the tender age of seven. 'Mind?'

'If it's usually locked then isn't it his? That's what I was told—that all locked areas are private, for the royal family only.'

And that was when he realised what was odd about this conversation. There was no awe in her expression, no hesitation in her manner because she had no idea who he was. Laurent could not remember the last time that had happened—if indeed it ever had. True, he'd been helping shift furniture in the throne room and hadn't changed out of his oldest jeans, the ones that made his mother sigh on the rare occasion she saw him in them. His hair wasn't neatly combed but falling into his face, and his short-sleeved shirt was covered with dust. No one expected to see an Archduke look like one of the many labourers working away to make the palace perfect for the ball of a potential billionaire fairy godfather. For one moment he was tempted to pretend that he was one of them, to enjoy this pomp and ceremony-free moment a little longer.

He pushed the enticing thought aside. Surely she'd wonder how a palace workman could give her permission to be in a private place and, besides, such games were beneath him.

He held out his hand with the straight-backed formality that had been drilled into him since before he could walk. 'I didn't introduce myself. I'm…' But the words were thick in his throat. Oh, he had a few, a very few, handpicked friends, men he could trust, who he could be some semblance of normal with for a few precious hours a week, but even with them there was an unspoken acknowledgement of his rank. When had he last had a conversation this free and easy?

He liked the frank way she chattered on, despite her embarrassment at having been caught trespassing. That would disappear in an instant once he revealed his identity. 'I'm...' But before he could complete the introduction Pomme came bounding over, his interest in the pretty stranger clear.

'Hello, beautiful, who are you?' Emilia bent over and found the exact spot behind Pomme's ears where he loved to be scratched. Laurent grinned as he watched his dog writhe with no self-consciousness whatsoever. 'What glorious colouring. Almost calico.'

'Pomme is an Armarian Spaniel. Originally bred to be hunting dogs, but he's a pampered pet, aren't you, Pomme?'

'He's absolutely gorgeous. Does he belong to you?'

'Yes. As you must have realised by now, he's Pomme and I'm Ren...' The diminutive came easily to his tongue. And it wasn't a lie; a very few people shortened Laurent to Ren. But never in public.

'Hi, Ren.' She straightened, one hand still buried in the dog's thick ruff. 'It was nice meeting you but I'd better go before we both get into trouble. I get the feeling the Archduke wouldn't be too happy if he caught me here.'

'I'm sure he wouldn't mind.'

'Maybe not. But I'd still better go. It was lovely meeting you. And thank you for not arresting me!' And with one last pat for Pomme, a smile that didn't quite reach her eyes and a swish of her ponytail she turned and walked away. Laurent stood in the shadows and watched her walk out into the sunlight, the solitude he'd been craving suddenly not feeling as desirable as it usually did. 'Emilia,' he said softly, tasting her name, before heading over to the arbour to finally read the report that would help him save his country.

CHAPTER THREE

THE MOMENT OF stillness before an event took shape was always Emilia's favourite time. She loved the second an event became a success, of course, watching her hard work come to fruition. And she adored the exhilaration that always greeted a finished event. The knowledge that once again all her hard work, long hours, last-minute decisions and substitutions and occasional panics were worth it. But stepping into an empty space for the first time, visualising it filled with people, mentally dressing and decorating and transforming it, was always the best bit of the job. She'd created wonderlands out of bland conference rooms, fairy tale backdrops from ordinary gardens and come up with more innovative conferences than any one person should have to organise in one lifetime and they all started here: gazing out at a blank canvas, pure and mistake-free.

Of course her blank canvases weren't usually eighteenth century ballrooms, large enough to hold several hundred people, with doors leading to ante rooms, dining rooms and private nooks. They didn't usually have a wall of French windows leading out onto exquisite balustraded terraces. She would have to be a poor event planner indeed not to create the perfect ball with this backdrop, even with two very different but potentially demanding clients and just three weeks to work her magic.

On the one hand was her father's sixtieth birthday. Simone had emailed Emilia several lists of demands, from a wish for her father's favourite music and food to be included to a command for a themed ball. At the same time it was clear that, although the Midsummer Ball hadn't been held for over two decades, the night itself was an important one in the Armarian calendar and there were many traditions that had to be incorporated into the event, from country dances to a candlelit procession and special flower wreaths for unmarried women.

Tablet in one hand, tape measure in the other, Emilia started to examine the room, taking pictures of possible breakout and bar areas, and pacing out where the stage might be. The minstrels' gallery would be perfect for a small band but not for a full orchestra and other music acts needed for the dancing section of the ball.

The royal family had evidently taken the upcoming event as an excuse to freshen up the castle. Every corridor echoed to the whines of drills or the banging of hammers and the smell of paint and turps was omnipresent. Stepladders, ladders and stools were propped up in every corner and dust sheets shrouded paintings and statues. It was all a reminder of just what a big deal this ball was. A career-defining ball.

But, more than that, it was an opportunity to give something personal to her dad, something only she could give. He might not recognise her hand in the evening and she probably wouldn't even speak to him or acknowledge that she'd been involved in any way, but making his birthday special might be a way to...what? To make amends for her role in their estrangement.

At first she had blamed only him—well, her father and Simone. But with maturity had come a painful understanding that her own behaviour had by no means been beyond reproach. Hurting from her parents' divorce, grieving for her beloved *maman*, torn away from her home, she had retaliated with the only weapons she'd had—her tongue and her rebellious spirit. And what weapons they had been.

If only things had been different...

Closing her eyes, Emilia took a step and then another, whirling around as if she were in the middle of the ball. In another universe she wouldn't be an employee; she'd be the daughter of the guest of honour. She'd dance with him on his birthday, she'd dance with the Archduke; their names would be linked but she would laugh the rumours off because she would be more interested in working in her father's business than in marrying a public figure. At this ball she could smile and laugh with no regrets and her father would have no reproach in his eyes. There was no Simone, no Bella…

Abruptly Emilia stopped and opened her eyes. Daydreams were just that. Dreams. Inconsequential, useless. She needed to push them aside and concentrate on the ball. It was all she had.

The whole castle hummed with activity and optimism and Laurent found he was humming along with it. Usually his role demanded a certain distance and formality but it was all hands on deck to ensure that the castle would look its very best under the spotlight of the world's media. For the last few years many of the staterooms had been a little neglected as they were only open to tourists on one day a week, a multitude of cracks and faded plasterwork hidden by closed curtains and strategic lighting. Any formal receptions were held in the wing of the castle which hosted the country's parliament and, as a result, it was immaculate. It was nice to see the older rooms come back to life, just the way they had been when his father was still alive and Laurent was allowed to be just a little boy, not the Archduke, bowed by duty and expectation.

Pomme by his side, Laurent half jogged towards the ballroom. It wasn't often he got to do really practical things, despite a youth spent in the Army cadets and two years before university spent training as an officer. He might be able to create a bivouac out of three branches and some leaves, light a fire using flint, forage for and cook his own dinner and use every gadget on his army knife correctly, but he didn't get many opportunities. When he was in the castle his food was cooked and served to him, his baths run, his clothes laundered, put away and laid out. People's jobs depended on his inertia. It didn't make said inertia any easier to bear. But right now there were more jobs than people to do them and not only was he back in the disreputable jeans usually worn strictly in private, but there was a ladder and a tin of paint with his name on. Turned out this ball was a good idea after all.

Reaching the ballroom, Laurent skidded to a halt, Pomme one step behind. The room was already occupied by a slight brown-haired girl, twirling around at the far end, arms outstretched as if she were waltzing. Emilia. His chest tightened as he watched her turn, an almost overwhelming desire to walk over and take her hand, be part of her dance, enveloping him. Her eyes were closed, her expression unsmiling but serene, as if she were many miles away, in a different time and place. And then her arms dropped, she stilled and her eyes opened, her face dark with a melancholy and emptiness that Laurent recognised. A look he occasionally saw in the mirror but had never seen on another person's face. It made him profoundly un-comfortable, as if he were trespassing somewhere he had no right to be, and he stepped back, intending to make a noise as he re-entered the room and give Emilia warning of his proximity. But, somewhat inevitably, Pomme had different ideas. Recognising the person who gave such excellent ear rubs, he bounded past Laurent and, with a snuffly woof, collided with Emilia's legs and thrust his head under her hand, tail wagging at a speed of at least a hundred beats an hour.

'Pomme!' Laurent called, half amused, half exasperated by his dog's manners—and a little bit jealous. How nice to be so confident of your welcome by such a pretty girl—and so justified in that confidence, he thought, watching Emilia bend her knees in order to get closer to the squirming, happy dog. 'I do apologise. He has had training but he forgets himself when he sees a friend.'

Emilia looked up at that and an expression of such utter joy passed over her face that Laurent nearly took a step back. She had a thin, rather solemn face, dominated by huge hazel eyes, but when she smiled it transformed from prettiness to a very real beauty, her eyes lit by gold flecks, her full mouth set off by identical dimples punctuating her cheeks. 'Am I his friend?'

'He seems to think so.'

'My first Armarian friend. And what a handsome one.'

'He knows it too,' Laurent said drily. 'I try to limit compliments to one a day, otherwise he gets a swelled head.'

She laughed at that and he was conscious of pride at her reaction. He sensed she didn't laugh often. 'You have more self-control than me. If I had a dog like this I would spend my whole time telling him how gorgeous he is and just what a good boy.'

'You don't have a dog? I assumed you did; you have the magic touch.'

'No—' she straightened and the light left her eyes as if it had never been '—I had one when I was very little but when my parents split up...' She didn't finish the sentence.

There was a world of unhappiness in the unsaid words. 'Everyone should have a dog.'

Laurent was hit with inspiration. 'In fact Pomme is the proud father of a new litter. You could have one of his puppies as a souvenir of your time here.'

'You fathered a litter? What a clever boy.' Emilia addressed Pomme in caressing tones. 'But I couldn't possibly. I mean, his puppies are bound to be expensive. And I live in London. But thank you. That's a lovely thought.'

'Well, if you change your mind...' Laurent didn't know why it was so important to him, but he vowed to make sure that when Emilia left she took a puppy with her. A girl who obviously loved dogs like she did should have one. Sometimes it felt as if he could only really be himself with Pomme and he couldn't help guessing that she was similar; again he felt that odd sense of intimacy, as if he already knew Emilia, as if they were alike.

He shook the thought away. A smile and a quick conversation and he was making up a connection that couldn't exist, projecting his own feelings onto a strange girl because of a luminous smile and the sadness in her eyes.

'Don't tempt me; it wouldn't take much to change my mind, but it wouldn't be fair. A dog like this wants countryside and freedom, not city parks and bylaws. Besides, I share my home with two other girls and I have no idea what they'd say if I came home with a puppy. But it was a very kind suggestion.'

'Don't make your mind up completely until you've seen them. In fact, what are you doing now?'

'Measuring and planning. I'm thinking that with such disparate ages and types of people attending the ball it might be fun for several different bands to play concurrently and other entertainment to be on offer as well. Like a grand fete or a fair, a kind of festival vibe, you know? Make the gardens an extension of the ballroom, especially for the more traditional elements which feel like they belong outside. Apparently there are several marquees we can use and plenty of outside staging. At least the weather is pretty much guaranteed to be warm and dry, a definite bonus. In London we always need rainy day contingency, even—especially—in the height of summer.'

'Sounds good.' It really did—and refreshingly different from the balls of the past, grand formal occasions accompanied by the swelling tones of the orchestra, of waltzes and foxtrots, the gardens a mere backdrop and place for assignations. But this was a new start, a fresh dawn for a new Armaria, and Laurent couldn't help but be entranced by Emilia's vision—and by the animation in her voice, her face, in her whole body as she described it.

'I hope so. I have to run my ideas past the Contessa, and past Simone tomorrow. Unfortunately, they don't seem to actually speak so everything has to be conveyed through me. Luckily, there's a big enough budget and enough space to accommodate everyone's ideas, but I haven't broken it to the castle staff that Simone would like a themed ball—complete with costumes. I'm not sure how the Archduke and Duchess will feel about that.'

'Nor am I.' Laurent spoke with perfect truth. He suspected his mother would hate the idea but accept it philosophically if it helped them achieve their objectives. He, on the other hand, would do anything not to add to the little furrows creasing Emilia's forehead as she spoke. 'But the ball is in honour of Mike Clayton so I'm sure they will be happy to accommodate his wishes.'

'I hope you're right. I managed to talk her out of fairy tales and medieval knights but I need to offer her something in return. I was wondering...' She paused.

'Yes?'

'Well, I know Shakespeare is English but he's kind of universal and lots of his plays are set around here. I was wondering about *A Midsummer Night's Dream* as a theme? Then people can wear pretty much what they like—go traditional in Greek chitons or Tudor clothing or anything else really. It fits in really well with the traditional Armarian wreaths and we can supply masquerade cloaks and masks for anyone who doesn't want to dress up. I thought we could hire actors to perform the play, just wandering the grounds.'

'Sounds like a great idea; I must get a donkey's head ordered immediately.'

'You'll be attending the ball then?'

'Yes…' Laurent remembered with a sinking feeling that he hadn't actually told Emilia who he was. 'I hope you'll save a dance for me.'

'Oh, I won't be dancing. There's always too much to do behind the scenes. My costume will involve trainers, black clothing so I can pretend to be part of the scenery and an earpiece. Not very glamorous at all. Less Titania, more a rustic. So what are you and Pomme up to now?'

Laurent nodded at the ladder. 'I'm painting. Pomme is waiting for me to finish so he can have a walk. He's not really any use at practical tasks.'

'It's amazing how hard everyone is working to get the castle ready. I mean, with candles and moonlight it would look incredible, but with all this buffing up it's really going to shine. I guess Mike Clayton really is important to Armaria.'

Laurent stilled. Was his wooing of the tech tycoon so obvious? 'What have you heard?' he asked, trying to keep his tone light as if the conversation was inconsequential.

'Not much, just that Clay Industries is looking for a new European headquarters and Armaria wants to encourage industry. You don't need an MBA to put two and two together and guess that this ball is a way of wooing them. Plus Amber said—' She stopped abruptly, her rather sallow cheeks turning pink.

'Amber?'

'My business colleague. She mentioned that there's a lot of chatter about the Archduke's marriage. Poor guy. Can't be much fun having the world's media watching your every move and speculating every time you speak to someone with working ovaries. Anyway, Amber said some of the gossip magazines are suggesting a closer tie than a business one between the palace and the Claytons.' She stopped, the pink now deep red. 'But I don't want to gossip; it's none of my business,' she finished, an odd, slightly bitter note in her voice.

'It's all right. You won't get arrested for gossiping about the Archduke's marriage. If it were a prosecutable offence half of Armaria would be in jail right now.'

'How horrid for him. I'm glad I don't have to deal with all that, aren't you? Even this glorious castle wouldn't make up for the lack of privacy and freedom. I've never fancied being royal or in the public spotlight. Not since I first saw *Roman Holiday*.'

'Since you went to Rome?' Laurent was slightly reeling from how accurately Emilia had summed up his situation. Most people told him how lucky he was, seemed to envy him the accident of birth that had placed him here. They didn't feel sorry for him or, if they did, they hid it well. It was bizarrely refreshing to hear such a different perspective.

He needed more of that. Fewer courtiers and advisers, more straight talking.

'No, I've never been to Rome, although one day I would love to, not that that's relevant. No, I meant *Roman Holiday*. The film. You must have seen it. Audrey Hepburn? Gregory Peck?'

'An old film?' His mouth quirked in amusement, his smile widening as he watched Emilia bristle.

'A classic,' she corrected him.

'So no high-speed chases?'

'You need to watch more classics; there's plenty of high-speed chases in them. *North by Northwest*, *To Catch a Thief*, anything with Cary Grant.'

'But not in *Roman Holiday*.'

'No, but there is a scooter. I can't believe you don't watch classic films; you're missing out.'

Laurent leaned against the wall and folded his arms, Pomme coming to sit by his side. 'Let me guess. It's set in Rome and—who is it, Audrey Hepburn?—she's on holiday and

meets an Italian millionaire played by Cary
Grant and they don't like each other and then
they fall in love. On a scooter.'

Emilia crossed her own arms in response
and fixed Ren with what he assumed was
her most withering glare. It was actually
pretty adorable and his chest tightened again.
Standing here, faux arguing, just hanging
out with an intelligent, beautiful woman as
if he were no more than the handyman she
thought him was the most fun he'd had since,
well, since he could remember.

'You couldn't be more wrong,' she said
loftily. 'It's Gregory Peck for a start and he's
American, not Italian, and a journalist looking for a big story.'

'My favourite kind,' Ren murmured. He
couldn't quite keep the dryness out of his
voice and Emilia glanced at him uncertainly.

'She's a princess in Rome for some big
summit and she sneaks out of the palace for
a bit of freedom.'

'That's more like it. I like the sound of her.'

'She's utterly charming. Very fragile but

regal as well, with these huge sad eyes.' Laurent couldn't help but feel as if Emilia was describing herself. 'Anyway, Gregory Peck recognises her and thinks he's going to get an exclusive so pretends he has no idea who she is and takes her on this whirlwind tour of Rome while his friend takes loads of photos of her. She cuts her hair and they see all the sights and then they fall in love...'

'Is there a happy ending?' For one moment he felt wistful yet hopeful, as if this wasn't the plot of a film but a true story which promised hope for his own predestined path.

'No, I mean, it's more bittersweet. She goes back and he turns up at the press junket and she recognises him and thinks her secret escape will be front page news, but he just looks at her—in this absolutely amazing heart-in-his-eyes way—and she looks at him in the same way, only discreetly, so the rest of the journalists don't guess, and he manages to give her the photos so she knows she's safe. And when she does her speech it's all aimed at him, like a love letter wrapped up in the formal part. That's the film that made me not want to be a princess. It was far more fun to ride with Gregory Peck and drink Prosecco in Rome than deal with dignitaries and probably marry some boring prince.'

'Quite right too. Who would want to marry a prince?' She glanced at him and he made his expression as guileless as possible. 'So that's the end? She goes back to do her duty?'

'I used to imagine a sequel,' Emilia confessed. 'Her kingdom had been turned into a republic and she was free to marry whoever she wanted. She meets Gregory Peck again as she's trying to start a new life and this time they can be together. Not that I'm usually a hopeless romantic. Just in this case.'

'Even princesses in exile are expected to marry into other royal houses. I wouldn't count on your princess getting the normal life she wanted, even after a revolution.'

'But not today, surely. I mean princes marry actresses and princesses marry personal trainers. The rules have changed.'

'Maybe,' he allowed. 'But an heir to the throne or a ruler cannot always follow their heart. Sometimes they have to do what's right for the whole country. Even in a place like this. Especially in a place like this.'

And, just like that, they were back to where they'd started. 'So you think it's true? The Archduke is going to marry Bella Clayton?'

'I think the Archduke will recognise what economic and business sense it makes to create close ties with a man who can bring such wealth and prosperity into a country which desperately needs something new.'

'That seems harsh on both of them. But maybe we don't know everything. Maybe they're head-over-heels in love.'

'Maybe.' It was definitely time to change the subject. 'Do you have time for a quick break? Let me introduce you to the puppies. Even if you don't want to adopt one, you should still meet them.'

'How can I resist a puppy break? Let me just measure out the stage first. Here, take this end of the tape measure and keep walking back until I tell you to stop. Ready? Okay, keep going…further, further. Right there. Great!'

Walking backwards, Laurent had no idea that anyone else had entered the room until he stopped and heard a voice behind him, his heart sinking as he heard the cultured tones of his mother's private secretary.

'Ah, there you are, Emilia. Her Royal Highness was hoping for an update. Would you be able to spare five minutes right now?'

Laurent wanted to keep his back turned, to allow himself another day, another few hours of being Ren the handyman, of being able to spend a few more moments teasing Emilia about old films and listening to her speak with complete candour. But he knew his time had run out and he had barely half turned before the Contessa had sucked in a breath and fallen into a curtsey. 'Your Highness. I didn't expect to see you here.'

Emilia looked across at him, shock and disbelief darkening her eyes. 'Your Highness?' The question was so faint the Contessa didn't pick up on it.

'Of course, if you are busy with the Archduke then I am sure the Dowager Archduchess will not mind a slight delay. I'll tell her to expect you in, say, half an hour?'

'No, it's fine. I think we're done here, aren't we, Your Highness?' And Emilia gave him the briefest of curtseys and left with the Contessa before Laurent had a chance to say a word. But what could he have said? His brief trip into normality was at an end. It was probably for the best.

But he'd enjoyed being treated like a normal human being, found the way Emilia had teased him more than just refreshing; it was like peeping into an alternative world, one where he was free to make his own friendships, his own path. To meet a girl and pursue the attraction.

Laurent had no idea what would happen after the ball, if he would find himself an engaged man or not—but he did know one thing. He liked the way Emilia made him feel and he wasn't ready to stop feeling. Not just yet. If there was any way to salvage this new friendship then he had to give it a try. He'd been raised to do his duty by his country and he had every intention of doing so. But he still had three weeks before things potentially changed for ever. What harm was there in spending some of that time with Emilia? He quashed the dutiful voice pointing out his desire to see Emilia again had nothing to do with friendship and far too much to do with how much he was attracted to her. He spent his life dealing with inconvenient truths. He was allowed the odd illusion.

'What do you think, Pomme?' he asked his dog, who cocked an ear attentively at the sound of his master's voice. 'Have I messed up altogether? You'd like to see Emilia again, wouldn't you?'

Pomme whined and Laurent gave him a rueful grin. 'You're right; it won't be easy and it's probably a bad idea, but for once I say let's not think about all the reasons why not. Deal?'

Pomme sat down, his tail wagging enthusiastically. It was all the answer Laurent was going to get, but it was enough. He wasn't giving up on this new acquaintance, not yet. And he knew exactly the way to tempt her.

CHAPTER FOUR

EMILIA JUMPED AS her phone trilled, startling her out of a daydream. Flustered, she fumbled to answer the call and, as she did so, noticed the name doodled on her notepad.

Ren...

God, she was a complete and utter fool.

'Hello?' She did her best to sound like the competent person she usually was, grabbing a pen and furiously scribbling out the doodled name, cheeks flushing hot as she did so. What on earth was she doing, randomly inserting the names of young men she barely knew into the middle of her to-do list? Acting as if she were some love-struck teenager doodling on her pencil case? She was neither love-struck nor a teenager. She was a professional, and she needed to behave like one.

'Emilia? Hi, it's me, Harriet. Just checking in. Is everything okay? You sound a little flustered.'

'Flustered? No, not at all. Just deep in thought. There's a lot to do.'

'How's it going? Met anyone yet?'

Emilia looked around, suddenly suspicious. What had Harriet heard? And from who? 'What do you mean, have I met anyone? Just because you're all loved-up doesn't mean everyone has to spend all their time thinking about romance.'

There was a startled pause at the end of the phone. 'Em! You know I didn't mean that. Have I turned into one of those people, the "everyone should get engaged" type, because you know I don't believe that…'

Damn it, now she had upset Harriet. 'No, no, of course you haven't. Ignore me. I was being silly.'

'You're sure?' Emilia couldn't blame Harriet for sounding hurt. The four friends had bonded through loneliness and they all found it hard to let people in, especially potential romantic partners. Harriet, like Emilia, had barely dated before she'd got engaged to Deangelo.

'Of course I'm sure.'

'I just meant have you spoken to anyone yet. Alex said you were buried alone in a basement office and sleeping in the attic. You should move to a hotel, Em. I'm more than happy to add it to Simone's gigantic bill. In fact, we'll get you a suite, champagne every night and fresh flowers and chocolates.'

'It's almost worth it just to imagine her face, but I'm fine here. Honestly, the office is perfectly adequate. Natural light would be nice, but it has everything I need, and the bedroom is clean and comfortable and has gorgeous views across to the mountains. It does me very well.'

'If you're sure…' Harriet still sounded doubtful and Emilia hurried to reassure her.

'Honestly, being here puts me at the centre of all the action and that's really important. You know I grew up bilingual, thanks to my mother? I barely use my French nowadays, but it's returned pretty quickly and I know enough Italian to manage to communicate well enough in dialect which, although everyone speaks English, they really appreciate. I've been helping out where I can; the whole palace is being overhauled, and it's paying off. Much easier to get people to cooperate with me if I've done them a favour first.'

'And what have you found out? Any gossip on whether the Archduke is going to propose?'

Emilia closed her eyes and saw Ren—Laurent—leaning against the wall, arms folded, blue eyes alight with laughter, disreputable old jeans moulded to strong legs like a second skin. He hadn't acted like an Archduke, nor a man considering marriage, two days ago.

But he was both.

'No, but everyone seems to think Dad's interest in moving the business here is a really good thing and they do seem to be taking it for granted that there will be an engagement within the year and Bella seems the most likely candidate. Apparently the Arch-duke has been to Dad's estate twice and Dad has visited Armaria, but the ball will be the first time Simone and Bella come here. I haven't told anyone what my relationship with them is. It's easier to keep work and complicated family life separate. Besides, everyone thinks Dad has just the one daughter,' she finished, trying to sound business-like, but Harriet wasn't fooled.

'You need to spend some time with your father, Em. It's his birthday. You have every right to be there.'

'I don't think that's entirely true.' Emilia blinked suddenly hot, heavy eyes. All she wanted, all she'd ever wanted, was her dad to put her first. But he never had. And the more she'd tried to get his attention, the more he'd turned away, pushing her to more and more extreme behaviour. 'After all, I threw my drink at him on his fiftieth and told him I wished he'd died instead of Maman. And then I walked out of the fancy restaurant, leaving him covered in lemonade. Not my finest hour—you can see why he wouldn't want me around on this occasion.'

'You were sixteen and hurting.'

'He didn't come after me though, did he? Not that night—not ever.' She swallowed, pushing the hurt back down where it belonged. 'He might be a genius but he has no emotional intelligence whatsoever. I guess that's why it was so easy for him to just walk out on Maman and me when he met Simone. If Maman hadn't died I doubt I would have seen him more than twice a year growing up, if that. He was always cancelling my custody weekends because he had to work or he and Simone had plans. Sent expensive presents instead, as if a new laptop made up for him not being there. The truth is neither Simone nor he ever bargained on me actually living with them and when I left it made their lives easier.'

'And yet here you are, on the spot for his birthday and Simone put you there. This is your opportunity, Em, your chance to talk to your father, to tell him how you feel. Okay,

I better go. This invoicing won't do itself, more's the pity. Call if you need anything, even if it's just a chat. Especially if it's just a chat.'

'Will do, thanks, Harriet.'

Finishing the call, Emilia wished she was the kind of person who could manage a casual 'love you' at the end of a sentence. But the words stuck in her throat. They made a person so vulnerable. She couldn't remember the last time she'd told someone that she loved them—or that someone had said those words to her.

Pushing the notepad away with a sigh, Emilia allowed herself to slump forward, head in her hands. It was all very well for Harriet to say this was her chance to talk to her father, but what would she say? She could apologise for her anger and behaviour as a teenager, but what if he didn't reciprocate? Still didn't see how he had let her down? After all, he hadn't tried very hard to reconnect with her over the last decade. What if she made herself vulnerable and at the end of it she still was on her own? All the hard work she had done to keep herself safe would be undone.

But watching Harriet deal with her father's dementia made Emilia yearn to at least try and put things right while she still had a chance. To be the bigger person, not the out of control teen pulling everyone into her maelstrom of misery. After all, whatever Simone's reasons for employing her, she had given Emilia the opportunity to show her dad how much she loved him. And, little as she had in common with her stepsister, to give Bella her due, she had always tried, inviting Emilia to lunches she was too busy to make, sending her gifts on her birthday.

But the thought of Bella brought her back round to Laurent again and Emilia groaned, grabbing her notebook and vowing to not think about anything but work again for the next two hours.

A rap at her door roused her from her thoughts and she called out for whoever it was to come in, surprised to see one of the pages carrying a silver tray with a brown envelope on it. The page, a boy in his late teens, wore the old-fashioned waistcoat and pin-striped trousers the role demanded with dignified pride.

'This is for you, *mademoiselle*,' he said in careful English, proffering the tray.

'*Merci.*' She smiled her thanks as she took the envelope, a little puzzled. The palace might have traditions and customs that seemed a thousand years old but behind the scenes it enjoyed the most up-to-date technology; the pages carried smartphones or tablets whilst Emilia had had no problem connecting to the palace's IT network. Who would be writing to her? Or—her heart speeded up as she felt something hard within the small envelope—sending her an object?

She began to open the envelope as the page left, tipping out a large wrought iron key. A tag was tied around the middle:

You are always welcome.

Putting the key onto the desk carefully as if it might explode, she reread the message, her heart thumping. It must be from Ren—Laurent. But why was he sending her an invitation to his private garden?

Sending her invitations, misleading her about his identity. What was going on? Emilia opened her top drawer and dropped the key and the message inside, closing it with a decisive bang. The answers to those questions didn't matter. She was here to do a job, not to speculate about the motivations of the Archduke. So he had sent her a key? She didn't need to use it. Her situation here was complicated enough. From now on she was steering clear of anything and anyone not related to the ball.

For the next twenty-four hours Emilia stuck to her resolution not to return to the walled garden, although she also didn't allow herself to speculate why she had retrieved the key from the drawer and stuck it into her bag, reading the note every now and then.

Instead she threw herself into an orgy of spreadsheets, Gantt charts and costings, cajoling or bullying her most trusted suppliers to agree to her impossible timeline. Whether it was Simone's lavish budget or the prospect of supplying the Royal House of Armaria she didn't know, but most capitulated far more easily than she had anticipated. In fact, they gave in so easily it took half the fun out of her job. Her mood only lifted when the palace head chef said an instant *non* to the menu she'd put together and they then embarked on a two-hour battle in which they both emerged convinced they'd been victorious. But throughout the feverish hours she was all too aware of the heavy key weighing down her bag.

By the following evening her head was aching after too much coffee and not enough air and Emilia found herself sent outside for a walk by the stately housekeeper with strict instructions not to return until her colour had gone from corpse to cream. She put up little fight, the need for fresh air almost overwhelming.

It was a gorgeous evening. Armaria was blessed with long hot summers, crisp snow-filled winters and springs and autumns out of a child's book of seasons and the early June evening was warm enough for Emilia to be out with no coat or jumper, the light not quite as bright as during the day, but still sunny enough to make sunglasses a must. She pulled the bobble out of her hair, allowing it to swing free past her shoulders, and took a deep breath, letting the fresh flower-scented air fill her lungs.

The castle gardens deserved all the accolades heaped on them. An eighteenth-century designer had created a visual masterpiece of terraces, fountains and colourful flowerbeds, the whole divided by trees and hedges, widening into more informal lawns and woodlands further from the castle. A maze at the foot of the terraces was known as the most fiendishly difficult in Europe, and the gardens were full of hidden nooks and secret corners. But as she wandered through the beautiful rose garden Emilia couldn't help but think about the walled garden, about how each plant seemed to be there naturally, not because it fitted some overarching vision, how the orchard trees wound and bent around each other, not pruned to unnatural symmetry. The garden was obviously tended, but it wasn't manicured.

And she had a key...

Of course she had told herself that going there would only lead to trouble. She had liked Ren. She might have only met him twice but she'd found him easy to talk to in a way that was unusual for her. In fact she'd been downright chatty. And although her life was a quiet one, she was still a warm-blooded woman. It was impossible not to notice that he was very attractive with his sudden, elusive smile and killer cheekbones. If Ren had sent her the key then, she would have been very tempted to visit the walled garden in the hope of meeting him there and seeing where their acquaintance took them. Tempted. Not that meeting strange young men was something Emilia habitually did. No dating apps for her, no accepting offers of coffee or dinner. Maybe she was a coward, but she knew all too well what could happen when you allowed your happiness to be held by someone else. That love had a toxic side, and not feeling at all was so much less painful than giving your heart only to see it disdainfully discarded. So no, she probably wouldn't have gone to meet Ren. But it was nice to think that maybe she would have summoned up the courage,

But *Laurent* had sent the key and she didn't know him at all. She would never have speculated about Bella and Clay Industries so freely if she'd realised who he was. And he hadn't denied that he was considering proposing to Bella, which made him doubly out of bounds and doubly dangerous—he had no idea who she was and her relationship with the man he so wanted to impress. So visiting the garden would be pure insanity and Emilia had only lived a sensible, planned existence since she had left home. This was neither the time nor the place to change that.

But as she neared the old wall set at the back of the castle, near the kitchen gardens which groaned under the weight of beds and beds of vegetables and herbs, Emilia was aware of a sense of an unusual and sweet anticipation and, before she knew what she was doing, she had unlocked the small door and slipped into the secret garden.

Disappointment dropped through her as she realised she was the only person there. 'Don't be silly,' she told herself, speaking aloud so as to give the words more weight. 'It's better this way; you can enjoy the garden with no awkward encounters.' Determined to do just that, Emilia explored every corner from the old orchard, buds turning to leaves, the promise of fruit heavy in the air, to the rambling roses which climbed the high walls and the beds filled with fragrant herbs and flowers. She discovered an old arbour housing an obviously much-used seat, the cushion dented with use, a blanket slung over the neck of the bench, and an archway leading into a shady courtyard filled with potted plants. No castle windows overlooked the courtyard; it was completely private, a small wooden door set into the castle the only clue it belonged to the castle at all and wasn't some magical garden in an enchanted land.

Despite the courtyard's privacy she felt uncomfortable being so close to the castle, the key heavy in her pocket, and after a quick peek she slipped back through the archway and into the walled garden, returning to her favourite tree, its branches providing a shady respite from the evening sun which still burnt with Mediterranean intensity.

Leaning against the trunk, she closed her eyes, aware the ache in her temple still hadn't quite disappeared, and breathed in the sweet evening air. It wasn't the work or the time pressure causing her sleepless nights and stress. It was knowing that she and her father would be occupying the same space for several days and that avoiding him for the whole time was unrealistic.

What if this ball was a sign that it was time to move on? To try and make amends. She wasn't foolish enough to imagine an ending where her father enfolded her in his arms and promised to make the last twenty years up to her, but she could walk away with her head held high, knowing she had done all she could. Maybe then she could finally move on. Find it within herself to be brave and search out the kind of happiness Harriet had embraced.

Her one attempt at a romantic relationship had backfired so horribly she'd steered well clear of any semblance of one ever since. But that had been a long time ago and she was older and wiser now. She had fought for and found her self-worth. Was she willing to let her father destroy it again? Especially now...

Her attraction to Laurent might be mis-judged and mistimed but it showed she wasn't made of ice after all. If she could let her guard down once then maybe she could again. Only next time she'd investigate any potential interest to make sure he was who he said he was and not the ruler of a small Mediterranean country.

'Is everything okay?'

She jumped at the sound of a low masculine voice, opening her eyes to see Laurent leaning against the tree next to hers, his eyes crinkled in concern.

'Oh, hi.' She was conscious of a bubble of happiness expanding her chest at the sight of him. 'I'm fine, but thank you.'

'Are you sure? Is there anything I can help with?'

The offer, from a man she barely knew, touched Emilia deeper than she wanted to admit. Was she really that starved for kindness? 'No, honestly. I only came here to return the key.' She slipped the heavy iron key out of her pocket and held it out to him. 'Here.'

Laurent made no move to take it. 'It's yours whether you use it or not.'

Emilia replaced the key in her pocket, half relieved he hadn't taken it, but not wanting to dwell on why. 'Why didn't you tell me who you are?'

His mouth tightened. 'That was badly done of me.'

'I said things I wouldn't have said if I'd known. I'm sorry. I overstepped...'

'Don't apologise. I put you in that situation. The truth is I liked the way you spoke to me; I liked the things you said. I liked the connection we forged.'

'Connection?' She could hardly breathe as she said the word and his eyes darkened.

'It seemed as if we already knew each other. Or maybe it was just me.'

Honesty propelled her forward until she was standing next to him, close enough to touch. 'I felt it too. But it wasn't real; it couldn't be real. You're not who I thought you were. You have a life I can't imagine, commitments I can't comprehend. A duty I respect and all that goes with that.' She didn't—couldn't—say Bella's name but it hung there all the same and in that instant she realised she was just as culpable because wasn't she too hiding who she was? If Laurent realised she was Mike Clayton's daughter then what—would he want to court her instead?

Maybe it was a big leap from connection to courting but, even if it was, Emilia knew she would never want to be wanted because of what she was instead of who she was. And maybe Laurent felt the same way. With that thought came a flash of understanding about why he might have withheld his identity from her, and with understanding came sympathy. She couldn't look at him as she spoke. 'But even if I do admit I felt a connection, the whole situation is too complicated.'

'Even in here? Where I am just Ren and you are Emilia and there are no titles and there is no duty or expectation? Can't we be friends here?'

'Well…' She was more tempted to agree than she would have thought possible. She was Emilia Clayton, who always played by the rules and buried herself in work rather than think about all the ways she wasn't living. But this garden felt like a place where those rules didn't exist and where Emilia could throw off those shackles and just be. 'I have to go,' she said instead. 'I'll miss staff dinner if I'm much longer.'

'In that case, why not stay here and have dinner with me?'

'Here?' She looked around as if food might spring magically up from the ground and a smile softened his rather harsh expression.

'Here. I'll be ten minutes. Promise you won't leave?'

'I...' If she walked fast she'd make it to the staff dining room before the end of dinner. She could slip into her usual spot at the end of the table and, as usual, eat a hurried meal, not really talking to anyone, her position too temporary and too undefined for her to easily fit in with the hierarchical castle staff. How tempting to agree to stay in this walled garden with a man who looked at her as if he knew her and liked what he saw, and pretend that the world outside the walls didn't exist. 'Okay, on one condition.'

'Name it.'

'Pomme joins us. I don't want anyone saying I ate dinner with the Archduke unchaperoned.'

His smile was as sweet as it was sudden. 'I'm sure that can be arranged. But inside these walls there is no Archduke, just Emilia and Ren. Deal?'

She couldn't help answering his smile with one of her own. 'Deal.' Staying was probably, definitely, a bad idea but she couldn't walk away even if she wanted to. Emilia wasn't one for crushes or sudden fancies; she wasn't really one for romance at all, for putting her body or mind or heart in the hands of another, trusting someone else with her happiness. She knew all too well how dangerous that was. But there was a flutter of sweet tension down in her belly when she looked at Laurent, a thrilling in her veins at the burr of his voice. He was still a stranger but at some level something in her recognised something in him. The unwanted, unasked for attraction should terrify her—and usually she would run from it—but here in this garden it felt natural. Safe. Even if she knew that safety was merely an illusion.

'Laurent?'

Laurent turned as his mother called his name, masking his impatience at the delay. It was seven-thirty and that meant Emilia would be in the walled garden waiting for him. The castle kitchens would have sent up a basket of food and it would be placed by the small door that led into the palace court-yard. If any of the staff wondered why the Archduke had taken it into his head to dine outside and alone every night for the past week, they kept it to themselves.

The evenings were an oasis during increasingly busy days. The Prime Minister was making his impatience felt and, although there was little he could do, he made sure Laurent knew just how little faith he had in the proposed deal and Laurent's ability to pull it off. The Chancellor's worry about the next year's finances were infecting all of Parliament and Laurent knew that if Clay Industries decided against investing then he would have to capitulate on some of the Prime Minister's demands. The ball and its outcome was increasingly important.

But during the summer evenings, stretched out on a picnic blanket, none of these concerns felt so urgent. Emilia was an entertaining and intelligent companion whose stories of her life in events often kept him amused for hours. Every evening he felt more at ease with her; every evening felt more and more like coming home.

Only real life kept intruding. Simone Clayton had suggested he and Bella wore matching costumes, a clear signal of intent from the Claytons and one he couldn't ignore. And a signal Emilia was aware of; she was organising the costumes after all. That was why, despite the intimacy of the situation, they never touched, never strayed into personal territory. The more time Laurent spent with Emilia, the more he liked her. The more he saw of her, the more he admired her. And he was definitely attracted to her. But he respected her too much to cross a line that once crossed would spoil the first real friendship he had experienced for far too long. A line a man contemplating marriage to another had no right to cross.

A line he wanted to cross more every night.

'Hello, Maman.' He kissed his mother's cheek as she approached him, smiling down at her. 'You're looking well.'

'So are you, *mon fils*. Is everything okay? I've hardly seen you all week.'

'I've been busy, with the ball, Parliament, arranging a tour for Mike Clayton. These things all take time.'

'Just a few days until they arrive and less than a week until the ball. Are you ready, Laurent?'

The truth was, three weeks ago he had been ready. Three weeks ago he had seen his path clear in front of him and known that following it was the right thing to do. But now he couldn't help but be enticed by other paths, winding, hidden paths with twisty corners and beguiling destinations. He set his jaw. 'Don't worry, Maman, I'm ready.'

His mood was sombre as he collected the basket and carried it through to the walled garden, an eager Pomme at his heels. Emilia was in her usual place, curled up under her favourite tree, her tablet in hand, forehead furrowed as she tapped away. She smiled as Pomme bounded over, one hand automatically caressing the dog's ears as she looked up at Laurent. 'How much would you hate traditional Greek costume?'

'A lot,' he responded as he placed the picnic basket on the ground, pulling out the blanket and throwing it over to Emilia, who caught it with one hand.

'Tudor dress?'

'No, thank you.'

'Regency?'

'For *A Midsummer Night's Dream*?'

'Breeches are timeless and it has to be better than a tunic. We're running out of time to get costumes made so you really need to pick one. Bella isn't keen on Tudor either but she is happy with either of the other two.'

'You pick.'

She looked up, startled. 'Me?'

'Yes, your event, you know what will work.' He knew he sounded autocratic, every bit the spoiled young aristocrat some thought him, and Emilia's expression was troubled.

'If you're sure. No complaining—if I put you in a pink frockcoat and a white wig you'll accept it?'

'If you put me in a pink frockcoat I'll have you arrested for treason.'

'Go with Regency,' she said, getting to her feet and shaking out the picnic rug. 'It's a classic for a reason and you and Bella can be Theseus and Hippolyta just as much as if you were in tunics. The flower wreath will still work with a regency hairstyle.' She bent down to pick up her tablet and began tapping away again and Laurent watched her.

He knew every bit of her now, the way she moved, the way her eyes turned from green to gold to brown to match her moods, the way the light caught her hair, bringing out honey highlights, the shadows that darkened her expression when she lapsed into thought, the dimples that peeped out when she was amused. He knew how she never stopped, her tablet always by her side as she made notes, answered emails and researched ideas even as she ate. How she rose early and worked late, how she already knew every inch of the castle and had ideas to showcase every one of those inches.

But he knew nothing about her background or her family. Had no idea if she had ever been in love. Her secrets were locked up tight and he had no right to go prying. Not while he was planning to go to his ball with another woman on his arm. Not while he was still planning to propose to another woman.

Not while his country's prosperity could depend on that proposal.

Maybe these evening picnics were a bad idea. He saw them as his salvation but he had been content with his path before Emilia had turned up.

But in just a few days Bella Clayton would be his guest and, regardless of what that meant, he would have to give her the courtesy of his time and attention. Their picnics had an end date. The thought pulled at him. This friendship couldn't just fizzle out. They should do something special first.

'We should do something different tomorrow evening,' he said and Emilia put her tablet down and regarded him in some surprise.

'Like what?'

'We could leave the castle while we can, before the ball guests arrive and your time becomes even more hectic. Let's hit the city. Where is your favourite place in San Tomare? The Italian quarter? The docks? The old town?'

Emilia's gaze shifted. 'I...well, I haven't had much of a chance to explore Armaria, not even the city. I've been so busy here, I haven't actually left the castle.'

'Not at all? You're not working twenty-four hours a day, surely?'

'No, but I am working all waking hours.

Three weeks is not very long to put on a ball, especially one where most of the guests need travel and accommodation sorting as well.'

'Then tomorrow I will show you my city.'

Every instinct screamed at him that this was a bad idea. These illicit picnics were one thing; a night out, beyond the safety of the castle walls, was quite another. But Laurent needed one night before his life changed for ever, a night when he wasn't Laurent; he was Ren showing the city he loved to a pretty girl.

'You want to show me the city?'

'People pay good money for guided tours, and I am offering you one for free. It's a one-time offer though…'

'Then how can I resist? Thank you.' She smiled then, that sudden full smile which transformed her thin, solemn face into something else entirely, into an enchanting beauty of curves and dimples, of hints of fire and a sweetness which took his breath clean away. 'That's very kind of you.'

'Not at all.' He managed to somehow keep

speaking although he wanted to stop time and drink her in. 'You're the kind one to take pity on me and grant me the pleasure of your company.'

She laughed at that, the usually hidden dimples deepening. Her laugh was husky, a little uncertain, as if she didn't unleash it often. 'I'll do my best to live up to that. Shall we meet here? Same time as usual?'

'No,' he said quickly. The last thing he wanted was for the soldiers who guarded all the entrances in and out of the palace to see them together, linking Emilia's name to his, exposing her to any resulting gossip. 'I'll pick you up at the crossroads, about quarter of a mile from the castle, if you go right when you leave the gates. Wear trousers, jeans if you have them, and a jacket,' he added and she stared at him, eyes wide with surprise. 'Sensible shoes are probably a good idea too.'

'Intriguing.' With that she opened the picnic basket and passed Laurent a perfectly chilled bottle of beer, taking one for herself as she did so. She raised hers to his. 'To new adventures.'

'To new adventures,' he echoed. But he knew that tomorrow wasn't about the new. It was about saying goodbye. To the old Laurent, to his old life and to the brief, sweet friendship that had so unexpectedly come his way.

CHAPTER FIVE

EMILIA SWIVELLED IN front of the narrow mirror. If she contorted and squinted she could just about see two-thirds of herself and that would have to do. Not, she reminded herself, that it mattered what she looked like. Going out with Laurent was a monumentally stupid thing to do. She'd allowed all those friendly evenings in the orchard to lull her into a false sense of security, but just because they'd fallen into an easy companionship didn't mean she could or should go out with him on the kind of evening that could be construed as a date.

Number one, he was an Archduke and she was an event planner from London who still shared a house with her friends. Her place was in the basement and the attic, not the ballroom. Number Two, he hadn't denied the rumours that he was going to marry another girl. Not just any girl: her own stepsister. A little fact she was keeping from him.

Their friendship might seem easy but it was based on evasion and half-truths and she was just as much to blame. And now it was going to be very difficult, if not impossible, to tell Laurent that she was the daughter of the man he was attempting to woo and the stepsister of his potential bride. Difficult and awkward.

Apart from anything else there was the small matter of the reconciliation she needed to attempt with her father. If Bella really was considering agreeing to be Laurent's Archduchess then nobody would be impressed if Emilia was seen swanning around with her stepsister's soon-to-be intended. They would assume that Emilia had done it on purpose, another attempt to grab the limelight and ruin her dad's birthday. No one would believe her friendship with Laurent was pure coincidence. Or innocent.

She wasn't too sure about the innocent part herself, even though they were both working very hard to keep it that way.

So the sensible thing to do would be to stop the evening picnics and stay home tonight with a box set and a box of chocolates. And Emilia could always be counted on to be sensible.

Couldn't she?

She looked down at her carefully chosen outfit. To be fair, nobody had actually said anything about a date. Tonight was a city tour—and she had been instructed to dress sensibly, which was not usually the precursor to anything romantic. So, sure enough, here she was, in a pair of jeans, trainers and a pretty flower-covered short-sleeved shirt, hair coiled up in her favourite messy bun, just enough make-up to look as if she wasn't wearing any. She was the epitome of 'just threw this on and yet somehow I look casually chic', a look that required forethought and ingenuity.

Forethought that would be wasted on dinner in the castle's staff dining room.

And, after all, she hadn't had an opportunity to explore the world-famous city of San Tomare yet and once her family arrived in just a couple of days it was unlikely she would find the time to eat, let alone explore.

Besides, there was nothing romantic between Laurent and her. Okay, to the untrained eye a week of picnic dinners in a walled garden might look like romance, but their hands had never so much as brushed together, they never held each other's gaze too long, and they hadn't spent their time together unburdening their souls. Emilia might not be that experienced in relationships but surely they couldn't—shouldn't feel so easy at the beginning, as if they had always known the other person? Shouldn't she be tongue-tied and overwhelmed, not so at ease she felt as if she might say anything and be understood? And all right, her heart might thump a little harder when she saw him, her palms tingle and her throat dry up.

She might sometimes allow her gaze to dwell on his wide shoulders and long, muscled legs and allow herself to daydream about the shape of his mouth, but Laurent was absurdly handsome and she was young and single. It would be weirder not to be attracted to him. It didn't mean he was attracted to her. He liked her because she wasn't deferential, because she treated him like just a normal human being, not a deity.

So what was she so afraid of?

She spent her whole life fearing rejection, worrying she wasn't good enough, that she didn't deserve happiness. She hid away, avoiding all opportunities, reasoning that it was far better to be safe than sorry. What had happened to that teenage firebrand who said what she thought and didn't care who got caught up in her wake? It had scared her, the anger, the way it had consumed her, the havoc she had wrought, the things she had said. And in the end hadn't she been the one to suffer? The one who ended up a teenage dropout, with no formal education, no family she could rely on, making her own way in the world.

She'd woken up the day after her father's fiftieth and taken a good, hard look at the last four years—and she'd been ashamed of what she'd seen. So ashamed that she had promised herself she would change, that from now on she would be calm and hardworking and always in control. And she'd achieved that, but at what price? She hadn't just dampened her spirit down; she'd extinguished it completely. Was this how she wanted to live the rest of her life? Maybe she should just make a leap of faith and let tonight just be. No planning or worrying or thinking about the worst thing that could happen...

Right. She was going to do this. *Carpe diem* and all that. Grabbing her light jacket and shoulder bag, she marched out of her small but functional attic bedroom and down the several flights of winding back stairs until she came to the small side door through which she accessed and exited the castle. She showed her pass so she could be signed out, took a deep breath and stepped outside. She was doing this. She was really doing this.

It took longer to walk down the imposing driveway than it did to amble along the flower-filled roadside verge until she reached the crossroads where she had arranged to meet Laurent. Like everything else she had seen so far in Armaria, the crossroads had an old-world charm exemplified in the wooden road sign, which looked like something out of a fairy tale, with its white paint and curling script. Feeling a little foolish, Emilia propped herself next to the sign and waited, unsure of the right posture to pull off *I only just got here* nonchalance.

The evening was still lovely and warm, verging on hot. Slipping off her jacket, Emilia inhaled the sweet, fragrant air which bore little relation to the heavy, fume-filled air she breathed every day on the streets of London. Rural idylls certainly had their place. Closing her eyes, she tilted her head, letting the evening sun bathe her face, enjoying the prospect of just being for once. Apart from the stolen hour she spent each evening in the walled garden, Emilia had barely stopped since Simone had dropped in so unexpectedly. In fact she had barely stopped since they'd opened the agency, or indeed since she had turned sixteen and realised that the only person she could rely on was herself. Working hard was in her DNA but right now she was prepared to allow herself a few moments to slow down and smell the—well, whatever the flowers were—and take in every sensation, like the buzzing of a bee, for instance. A buzzing that seemed to be getting louder and louder...

Emilia's eyes snapped open as the buzz sharpened to a roar. Either that was one huge bee or... She stepped back as a sleek motorcycle swooped down upon her, stopping with a stylish turn. The rider, dressed in black to match the bike, she noted, swung one lean, muscled leg round in order to dismount, pulling the helmet off his head as he did so.

Laurent.

'Hi, you're here!'

Emilia was absurdly flattered by the frank pleasure in his smile. 'I almost thought better of it,' she confessed. 'But I wasn't sure what the penalty was for standing up an Archduke. I didn't want the guards to be put to the trouble of dragging me here.'

His smile ratcheted up a notch and Emilia's breath caught in her throat. 'I was hoping you'd come willingly.'

'On that?' She eyed the motorbike sceptically.

'It's quite safe.'

'Hmm.' But she couldn't help the thrill that ran through her at the thought of riding pillion, her arms around his waist, legs pressed to his. Emilia swallowed, convinced her thoughts must be showing on her face. The problem with not dating for several years was that it left a girl with no defences; she was as new to this kind of banter as a fifteen-year-old with a crush.

'Here.' Ren went over to the motorbike and returned with a second helmet, which he handed to Emilia, who clutched it, her arms barely managing to contain it. It was heavier than she had expected. 'Ever worn one of these before?'

'No. And I'm not sure I'm going to do so right now either.'

'I promise I'll be really careful. And you never know, it might be fun.'

'It's a very big bike,' Emilia said doubtfully. 'I'd be more comfortable if it was one of those little pastel ones like in *Roman Holiday*.'

Ren merely raised an eyebrow. Of course he could raise just one eyebrow. And probably naturally; he didn't seem the type to practice in front of a mirror. She'd practised but never quite got the hang of it, much to her disgust. A sardonic raised eyebrow was much more useful than her dimples. They merely made her look cute, unthreatening.

She contented herself with matching his

expression, only with both eyebrows raised as high as she could manage. 'What?'

'We're back to old films again?'

'Have you watched it yet?'

'Not yet.' His smile was rueful. 'It seems a little too close to home.' Her pulse sped at his words, at the hint that Laurent wasn't as reconciled to his path as he seemed.

'In that case I should be the one driving the motorbike and taking you on the tour.'

'Maybe.' Laurent looked directly at her, expression unreadable. 'Do you think she regretted it? The Princess? Did her escape make her life more bearable or did she spend the rest of her days knowing she'd tasted freedom and longing for it?'

Emilia took a deep breath, trying to work out the right thing to say. 'It may have only been one night, but she lived every moment of it. I guess that's all we can ask, isn't it? An opportunity to really live, even if we know it's not for ever.' And as she said the words Emilia knew that she hadn't been living every moment, not even half. She had shut herself away just as much as Audrey Hepburn's Princess Ann. Only she wasn't hemmed in by custom and duty, but by fear. Fear of finding love and losing it, fear of mistaking something darker for love. It was so easy to believe that she wasn't worthy of love, after all; hadn't she been shown that over and over?

But Harriet and Amber and Alex loved her and they were the best people she knew. And Laurent was standing close to her, his eyes focused on her, looking at her as if she had the answers he was searching for.

'Is that what you think? That we should grab every opportunity while we can?'

When had he got so close? Emilia blinked as her body registered his proximity, heating up as she glanced up at him and saw the smile deep in his navy eyes. A smile and a glint of heat that sent her temperature ratcheting up yet another notch. Her stomach tumbled, a mixture of desire and fear.

But at the same time she didn't want to step back.

* * *

What was he doing? A ride into the city was one thing, a guided tour harmless enough, even dinner was innocent. But if he kissed Emilia then that would be quite, quite different. It would be dishonourable and an Archduke should always act with honour. So it was best to step away and try not to notice how full and inviting her mouth was, how soft. Best not to notice the dimples at the corner of said mouth and how they gave her usually grave features a lightness and sweetness. Definitely best not to comment on the length of her dark eyelashes, a deep brown touching on black, only with a hint of gold, a hint echoed in the flecks in her hazel eyes which right now were more green than brown.

Better not to notice how her breath hitched as their eyes locked and need shimmered in the hot evening air, how her jacket hugged her, nipping her in at her narrow waist whilst emphasising the curve of her hips and her breasts. No, definitely best not to think about her breasts.

But it was hard to think of anything else. The air was sweet with night blooming flowers and the subtle scent of her light perfume. Like a Mediterranean garden, a little citrus, a little floral, a little sea salt. She smelt like Armaria and right now was infinitely more desirable.

But he wasn't free. Not entirely. Because desire was one thing but duty another, and duty always came first. And so, reluctantly, he stepped away, nodding at the helmet she still cradled in her arms. 'Are you going to wear that or hug it?'

Her eyes flashed golden green. 'Wear it.'

It took a couple of moments for Emilia to figure out how to fasten the helmet but Laurent didn't quite trust himself to help her, ungentlemanly as leaving her to struggle might seem. The problem was that he didn't want to be gentlemanly or princely or Archduke-ish. What he wanted to do was pull that damn helmet off her head and kiss her until he forgot who and where he was. Until he was lost in her. He'd kissed more than a few women in his life and had never got lost in any of them, but none of them had been as potentially dangerous as Emilia.

He stepped back again. 'Are you managing?'

'Quite well, thank you.' Her voice was muffled by the helmet but her glare quite visible through the visor. 'Very comfortable. This isn't hot and uncomfortable at all.'

'Better uncomfortable and safe.'

Her eyes narrowed. 'You said you would be really careful.'

He couldn't help his mouth curving into a playful grin. 'I also said it would be fun.'

She froze for a second and he could see the indecision in every inch of her, until she tilted her chin. 'I'm ready.'

She might be ready but Laurent soon realised he wasn't ready at all. Not for the clasp of her hands around his waist, or her thighs wrapped around his, her breasts pressing against his back. It was torture, the kind that would entice a man to spill every secret and beg for more. Exquisite as it was, it drove him nearly out of his mind, his whole being surrounded by her.

It had been too long since he had been so close to a woman. Dating Laurent came with a whole set of rules and attention that put off all but the most determined women. Add in the likelihood that the couple would be followed by paparazzi wherever they went and her life and previous relationships scrutinised in depth and it wasn't that surprising that women often decided that maybe they weren't keen on being with him after all. After a few uncomfortable and too public attempts at relationships with fellow students in his early twenties, Laurent had all but given up, save for a brief, secret fling with an actress who valued her privacy as highly as he did and had no interest in marriage or a throne, and a longer, more public relationship with a minor member of the exiled Greek royal family which had faded away, probably due to his preoccupation with matters of state. But that was a couple of years ago and since then he had been on his own.

It wasn't much to look back on at the age of twenty-eight, with probable marriage looming ahead. Maybe he should have been more reckless with his own heart, if not with other people's. But it was nearly too late for regrets.

Nearly...

Laurent took a corner with a flourish and Emilia's arms tightened as the movement shifted her even closer. Usually he loved the freedom of the bike as he navigated the winding clifftop roads which connected the castle to San Tomare, green hills on one side leading to the mountains which separated his small country from the rest of the continent, the sea down below. He loved the roar of the wind, the kick of the bike, the knowledge that for these moments at least he was the master of his own destiny.

But this evening he wasn't just aware of the elements and speed, or ultra-aware of the feel of Emilia, of how close she was, but of how her safety was in his hands. The trust she was placing in him. He wrenched his thoughts away from the warmth of her body, grimly focusing on the road ahead instead.

For once he was grateful when the city outskirts forced him to slow down, and he cruised along until he finally pulled up outside a gated villa overlooking the sea in a cultural and tourist hotspot on the outskirts of the city. The popular suburb had so many second homes and holiday lets that no one speculated about the owner of the seemingly innocuous white-washed villa set back from the road. Slowing, he turned in, the sensor recognising him and the gates slowly swinging open, and he felt Emilia tense behind him as he rode the bike through the gates and they closed softly behind them. He pulled to a stop on the driveway which ran up the side of the villa and dismounted, holding a still gloved hand out to Emilia. She took it but only lightly, dropping it as soon as she was safely on her own two feet, already fumbling at the helmet, shaking her head as she removed it so her light brown hair tumbled free of the loose bun it had been confined in.

'Where is this?'

'The Villa par la Mer.'

'Which is?'

'My villa. I come here sometimes, when I need to escape. But today it's just a parking spot. San Tomare is the safest capital city in the world—safest and smallest—but I still prefer to keep my bike off the streets. Besides, this is the scenic way into town; if we walk through the gardens and onto the cliffs we then finish our journey by boat. Or we could walk through the streets or get a taxi. Up to you.'

'The sea way sounds lovely,' she said at last and smiled, a slow smile which gradually lit up her narrow face, her dimples flashing into view and giving her rather austere beauty a puckish charm.

'Okay.' It was hard to tear his gaze away from her, but he managed it, hoping he was looking cooler and more relaxed than he felt. 'This way.'

He didn't tell her that she was the first outsider he had brought here. That this villa was his sanctuary, a place he rode to on the rare occasions he could leave the palace. A place he invited no one to, not even his mother. But he knew Emilia would love it as much as he did. And, for reasons he refused to dwell on, he wanted to share this part of his soul with her.

The gardens weren't extensive, not as manicured or designed as the famous and formal castle grounds, nor as wild and free as the walled garden. Herb and vegetable beds ran down one side; the whole was shaded by lemon and olive trees, shrubs and flowers grew in large pots. The long garden was terraced as it led to the clifftop, walled off on both sides, the innocuous whitewashed bricks hiding the sensors and cameras which were the price Laurent paid for his occasional freedom. He pretended not to know that the villa on one side was owned by the castle and soldiers occupied it day and night and that the villa on the other was lived in by a now retired bodyguard and his formidable wife. The illusion of escape, of privacy, was better than no escape at all.

'Did you design the garden yourself?' Emilia asked as she followed him along the gravel path, pausing to touch one of the ripening lemons hanging enticingly at head height.

'No, my grandmother did,' he said. 'She was Austrian, descended from royalty on both sides and rich with it. The perfect Archduchess for a small impoverished country. But she was never comfortable in the spotlight. She told me once her dream was to live in a small village and be a housewife, maybe run a shop. Instead she spent her days entertaining diplomats and opening buildings.'

'How sad.'

'She didn't see it that way. She knew it was her heritage, her duty to marry well; she'd been raised to it. But she adored nature and the outdoors—the walled garden was her sanctuary in the castle, this villa her escape from it. She left both to me.' He smiled, remembering how his grandmother, always so regal and proper, came to life in her garden, wearing old slacks, her hair falling out of its chignon, her elegant hands covered in dirt. 'She was always happiest when she was out here, weeding or planting or pruning.'

Emilia turned slowly, her keen gaze taking in every detail. 'My mother was a keen gardener. Keen but not as talented as your grandmother. To be honest, I don't think she had much luck at all but it didn't stop her trying. She was French and so she blamed the English weather, said it was too damp and unreliable!'

'Was?'

'She died when I was twelve.' Emilia swallowed, looking for a moment like the grief-stricken child she must have been.

'I'm sorry,' Laurent said. 'I know what it's like to lose a parent when you're too young to make sense of it.'

'Of course you do. You were even younger when your father died.' Her voice was soft with an understanding few could really comprehend.

'Seven,' he confirmed. 'I think that's why I was so close to my grandmother. She, of course, had lost her son, and I think she found some comfort in me. But also my mother had to step up, to become regent, and everyone told me I was the Archduke now, that I had to be brave and grown-up. It was only here, with my grandmother, that I got to be a little boy and just run around and play.'

Emilia smiled at him then, with an infinite tenderness that warmed his heart and his soul. 'Thank you for bringing me here.'

'How about you?' They resumed walking, a slow amble down the path, Emilia stopping frequently to examine a plant or a statue or to smell a flower. 'Are you and your father close? It couldn't have been easy for either of you.'

She didn't answer for a long while, blinking slowly, the shimmer in her eyes a tell-tale answer to his question. 'We were close once. It's easy to forget that, because we aren't now. I sometimes wonder if I made up my memories of him from books, because I remember a happy home and a father who carried me on his shoulders and a mother who was always singing and a dog I adored...'

'And your mother's death changed all that?'

'No, it changed long before. My father moved out when I was six. He'd met someone else. She had a daughter, a year older than me, and it seemed like, felt like he had a whole new family and just didn't want the old one any more. My mum stopped singing and gardening; she was so bitter and angry. And Dad, well, I suppose he didn't want to face up to what he'd done so he stayed away from her, and that meant staying away from me. Of course, I thought it was my fault. That he'd left me because I had done something wrong. Part of me still thinks that...'

'That's nonsense,' he said quickly and she shrugged.

'I know. I told myself that then, I tell myself that now, but it just didn't seem possible for my dad, the man I absolutely adored, to just not be in my life for no reason. And the only reason I could think of was that I had said or done something to push him away. Or that Maman had. Anyway, Dad kept the London flat we'd lived in and bought a huge new house out in Surrey as well for his new family. Meanwhile, my mother and I moved to a poky area on the outskirts of London. He was—is—well-off, but Maman was determined to be independent, so we had a little flat with no garden and she got a job teaching French. The worst part was when she gave my dog to a friend who didn't work. She said it was fairer for him, that he couldn't be alone all day, and she was probably right but I missed him more than my dad—does that sound silly?' The wistfulness in her smile tore at his heart and all Laurent wanted to do was try and fix all her hurts.

'Not at all.'

'It was hard at first. I was sulky and resentful and she was so angry all the time, but after a while the new became normal and we settled in. She liked her job and made new friends and I got used to the fact that Dad would cancel our weekends together and on the few occasions I did see him we never got time alone; instead he expected me to make a happy family with his new wife and daughter. His wife never seemed keen on having me around and I was really resentful of her daughter, because she got to live with my father, have inside jokes with him, see him every day. I wasn't very nice to her, I'm ashamed to say. But then Maman got sick and she just didn't get better. Next thing I knew, I was living with the man who walked out on me and the people he'd left me for. I was so angry and so grief-stricken.'

'I'm sure they understood.'

She shook her head. 'I felt like my presence was an inconvenience. They just didn't know what to do with me, I suppose. I didn't want to go to my stepsister's fancy school; I wanted to stay where I was, even though it was a really long journey to get there. I didn't want to be part of their family or adapt to their ways. It felt like betraying Maman. The truth is…' she paused, taking in a long breath, her face unreadable '…the truth is, I suppose, if I'm honest, that I behaved very badly, rebelled every way I could. Made unsuitable friends, stayed out late and didn't tell them where I was, missed school. I even shoplifted a couple of times, even though the one thing I had plenty of was money. I wore clothes they hated and dyed my hair any colour I could think of. The irony is Maman would have been appalled. She was so chic and French, she would have wept when I cut my own hair. I just wanted them all to feel as hurt and guilty and lonely as I did, but the more I rebelled, the more alone I was. The next few years were hell. So I left home at sixteen, after doing my best to tear us all apart. But all I did was isolate myself; they were closer than ever.'

'You were a child who needed unconditional love and safety.' It was hard to rein in his anger. What kind of family allowed a newly motherless girl to struggle on alone? At least Laurent had always known his mother loved him, even if she was so busy all the time, and he'd had his grandmother. Turned out he'd been lucky.

Emilia sighed and it was the loneliest sound he'd ever heard; his heart ached to hear it. 'Now I barely see him. I lost both parents. That's what hurts so much. It took a long time to come to terms with that.'

'And have you come to terms with it?'

'In some ways. It helps that I made my own family.'

Surprised, he glanced at her bare left hand and she laughed. 'Not a conventional one. I don't think convention and I work too well. No, I made three very dear friends and we set up our own business. I know, no matter where they are, what they do and who they're with that they have my back and I have theirs. They understand, you see.'

'Understand what?'

'What it's like to have no one.'

The words were uttered so simply, with no self-pity or despair, just a matter-of-fact statement but one that chilled Laurent through. Without thinking, without giving himself time to second guess, Laurent put his arms around Emilia and held her close. He had no thought beyond offering comfort, although he couldn't help but be aware of the floral scent of her hair, of the softness of her breasts and the way she fitted against him, but he made no attempt to tighten his hold, to do anything but give her the warmth and support of another human being. To show her that she wasn't alone. And to realise that, for the first time in a long time, he wasn't alone either.

CHAPTER SIX

EMILIA EXTRICATED HERSELF from Laurent's embrace, unable to look at him. What on earth was she thinking? Why had she said all that? She had never opened up this much before, not even to Alex, Harriet and Amber. They knew part of the story, of course, but not the whole sordid tale.

Not only had she ended up confiding in him, but she had allowed him to comfort her as well, to hold her as if she were in need of looking after, of rescue. And Emilia knew better than to trust any of her happiness to others.

Only right now, standing on a shady terrace, the scent of lemons permeating the air, the sound of the sea crashing against the cliff creating an oddly musical backdrop, the evening sun shining down, the memory of his touch buzzing through every vein, it was almost easy to forget that she didn't believe in fairy tales—or in handsome princes. Easy to forget when a pair of blue eyes regarded her with such intensity, eyes belonging to a man with shoulders broad enough to lean against and the kind of mouth a girl could fantasise about, if she was the kind to fantasise, that was.

The silence stretched until she could almost feel it, tension strumming the air. She wanted to say something—anything to break it, but found she couldn't, held in his gaze. He was making a decision, she knew that. But what that was she had no idea. To kiss her? Like he almost had back at the crossroads? Emilia shivered, imagining how it would feel, that hard yet elegant mouth on hers, his tall body holding her close, maybe backing her against one of the lemon trees, the bark rough against her skin. Her whole body goosebumped at the thought and she swayed slightly, closing the distance between them with the movement of her body.

'Ready to continue? We're nearly at the clifftop,' Laurent said at last, his voice hoarse and a heat in his eyes that burned straight through her, lighting a trail that ran right down her body, liquid fire in every vein. Was this desire? Lust? She'd never allowed herself to feel like this before. Not with furtive kisses in the park in her teens, or her desperately needy kisses with her one and only proper boyfriend. Emilia knew better now; she didn't trust, not with her heart or her body.

Or she didn't usually. But right now her body was ignoring her bruised heart, her pulse racing with need, stirring up every nerve with its relentless thrum. She wanted and she needed. Had from the moment she'd been disturbed in the walled garden, had in every second since, every evening they sat together deliberately not touching until the air between them hummed with desire. She didn't believe in love at first sight and wasn't fool enough to believe this, whatever it was, *was* love. But that didn't make it less powerful, and stronger women than she had fallen under its thrall. She swayed again and felt Laurent's gaze follow every tiny movement, the roll of her hips and the curve of her breast and, with deep feminine satisfaction, she watched him swallow, her eyes following the working of his throat, taking in the dark blond stubble covering his jaw, the vee of hard chest exposed by his shirt, at once vulnerable and strong.

She spent her life working hard, as if that made up for never really feeling, never really needing. She didn't so much as live her life as make sure she was always far too busy to think. She didn't want to start thinking now. Think about why her next words might be a huge mistake. 'We *could* walk on. Or we could stay here. For a little while longer.'

His eyes narrowed as he seemed to take in every word and examine it. 'We could stay; it's a pretty spot,' he agreed. 'I could go back to the villa and get some wine if you wanted to stop here for an aperitif?'

'That sounds nice.' But she didn't need

Dutch courage—nor could she allow any time to elapse, not even the five minutes it would take to collect wine and glasses, otherwise she knew she would change her mind. No. She needed to act while she was still under this spell. It was Emilia's turn to swallow, with nerves, with anticipation, as she stepped towards him. 'Maybe later.'

He didn't reply, his mouth curving appreciatively although she thought she noted a hint of doubt cloud his expression, even as he visibly inhaled. She was affecting him. She was responsible for his preternatural stillness, for the way he watched her every move, half like a hunter, half like prey.

No, she amended as she looked straight at him and saw the way he seemed to be holding himself in check, the hunger in his eyes thrilling her even as part of her wanted to turn and run. She wasn't kidding anyone. He was all hunter.

But she wasn't anyone's prey.

She stepped again and then she was right next to him, almost within touching distance. She hadn't fully appreciated quite how tall Laurent was, how strong, despite his deceptive slenderness; every muscle was clearly defined. She was slim to the point of thinness and always felt angular, all corners, taller than her friends, yet looking up at Laurent she felt petite, delicate. Her jeans and shirt seemed girlish, feminine, *she* felt girlish in a way she had never felt before. If she'd been from a previous era she would be waving a fan right now in a deliberately provocative way.

As she stood there, mind for once at the urge of her body, Emilia remembered what Harriet had said about the moment she had thrown caution to the wind and kissed Deangelo for the very first time. *I was so tired of always being afraid. I wanted to really feel alive, just once.* Emilia bit her lip, the slight pain recalling her back to herself. She knew exactly how Harriet had felt. Knew exactly what it was like to live closed off and afraid and lonely. The last few months, she had begun to feel part of a family again, but

Harriet's engagement showed how fragile those ties really were. Oh, their friendship would last, she had no doubt about that, as hopefully would the business, but Harriet's life had expanded, even as hers contracted even further until work was all she had.

One kiss. What harm would one kiss on a sunlit evening in a garden filled with the scent of lemons do? If she just dared. After all, no one would ever know…

She moved a little closer, her whole body now humming with need and want, delicious shivers running down her spine, aware of every nerve and how it sang with excitement. Reaching out, she touched Laurent's arm, warm and solid under her fingertips. He stood still, but a quiver ran through him as his eyes darkened even further to the almost grey of a storm-tossed sky. Emilia looked directly at him, allowing her desire to show in her eyes, for once hiding nothing, swaying further towards him, lips parted, and with a noise that was half a growl, half a smothered curse he tilted her chin, looking down at her for a long second before his mouth found hers.

Emilia had been expecting a slow warm-up kiss, maybe something gentle and tentative, a getting-to-know-you kiss, but why should a kiss be any different from their acquaintance so far? Hadn't they jumped from *Sorry for trespassing* to dinners for two without passing Go or collecting two hundred pounds? From the moment his mouth claimed hers the kiss spiked straight to incendiary, his lips provoking sensations and feelings she hadn't even known existed. Her hand still lay on his arm but otherwise their bodies didn't touch and, much as Emilia wanted Laurent's hands on her just as much as she wanted to claim every inch of his tall, lean body, touch every sinew and muscle for herself, she also knew if she did she would be undone.

No, better to lose herself in the kiss, to let his mouth take hers, at once hard and yet tantalisingly soft. Let herself get lost in his taste, in the ripples of lust shuddering through her body, in a rhythm that felt so right she could dance to it.

They could have been standing there for thirty seconds or thirty minutes or even, lost as she was, for thirty hours, but when he lifted his head and broke the kiss, it hadn't been long enough. One kiss? Who had she been kidding? Pandora had opened the box and she wanted more.

'Emilia...' Laurent's smile was a little rueful, a lot satisfied and a tinge wolfish, a combination that reached inside her and tugged hard down deep. 'I didn't bring you here to take advantage. I hope you know that.'

'Actually—' she tried for blasé and a little provocative '—I think I was the one who took advantage of you.'

'Is that so?' His smile was all wolf now and she wanted nothing more than to submit, but she lifted her chin and matched his smile with her own.

'Don't worry,' she said kindly. 'I like that you're not intimidated by strong women.'

His eyes flared with heat and a challenge

she longed to answer, but his tone was cool and amused. 'That's good to know. What do you say, are you ready for that boat ride now?'

'Absolutely—lead the way.'

Emilia followed Laurent down the path, her head still dizzy with lust, her mouth full of the taste of him and yet in some ways it was as if the kiss had never happened. Laurent made no effort to hold her hand or slip an arm around her as they made their way through the garden, but there was a tension between them, a crackle in the air, electricity any time their hands or arms accidentally touched, that showed neither were as impervious as they might pretend. Neither spoke until they reached the clifftop. A low wall was all that stood between the end of the garden and dramatic cliffs, with the sea tumbling against the rocks below.

'Do we abseil?' Emilia stared down at the churning white water. 'Is that why you told me to wear comfortable shoes?'

He smiled at that and her heart flipped.

Princes shouldn't have such devastating smiles. It was most unfair.

'Not quite. Look this way.'

The tunnel was so cunningly hidden Emilia would never have noticed it on her own, the entrance concealed in a tangle of olive trees. A narrow steep slope led to a door, locked by an electronic keypad. Laurent led her down it, then punched in a long series of numbers and the door swung open. It was more like entering some vault than a path down to the sea.

'What is this?' The passage was tiled, the wall plastered and painted white. Lights were hidden in the ceiling illuminating the windy way down through the cliff. 'A smuggler's lair?'

'Once upon a time, yes. There was a time long ago when all of coastal Armaria were smugglers and pirates, but now it's just a simple shortcut to the beach.'

'Is it safe?' She wasn't scared of heights or claustrophobic but the thought of walking through a tunnel dug out of a cliff, surrounded on all sides by tons of rock, made her heart beat faster and her palms dampen with nerves.

'Completely. My grandmother used it for sea bathing well into her late seventies. But we can always turn around if you're nervous.'

'No, I'm fine.' She wasn't going to be outdone by a septuagenarian grandmother. 'Just a little surprised, that's all.'

'I'm full of surprises.'

Emilia peered into the tunnel. Ever since she had first met Laurent her life had turned upside down. She'd found herself daydreaming at work. Flirting with a strange man. Confiding in a strange man. Getting on a motorbike with a strange man. Kissing a strange man. Now she was preparing to follow said strange man into a tunnel, trusting the destination was as he promised, trusting she'd be safe. But if she hadn't been here, what would she be doing? She knew exactly what—she'd be sitting at her desk, updating her project plan and budget, answering her emails, checking the plans the temporary event planners she'd hired to cover her work back in Chelsea had submitted for her approval. Burrowing into work, putting all her hopes and dreams into work, just as she had every day since she'd walked out of her father's birthday party, all her validation confirmed with every word of thanks, of praise. It had been enough. It had been all she had.

But something had changed in the last few hours. She had changed. And there was no going back.

'Okay then.' She reached out and took his hand, the strength in every sinew flowing into her. 'Let's go.'

Laurent was an honourable man. He had to be. He'd promised on his father's deathbed to behave with honour and put Armaria first. But he hadn't been thinking about honour or Armaria when he kissed Emilia. He hadn't been thinking at all. He had been all instinct and need and desire.

Technically he was still free to kiss anyone he wanted. He had said nothing to Bella Clayton that was even flirtatious, let alone a proclamation, made no promises and asked for none in return. She had no hold on him and he none on her. But he still needed her father's company to invest in Armaria and he knew there was plenty of speculation linking their names; by agreeing to joint costumes at the ball he was making a statement of some kind of intent, subtle as that statement might be. Joint costumes and gossip didn't tie him to Bella Clayton. But while he was still considering proposing, honour should have stopped him kissing anyone else.

True, he knew that if he proposed and Bella accepted, then she wouldn't be doing so in any expectation of love. No, she would be marrying him for position, as men and women had married for centuries. But she would have a right to expect her husband's respect, his fidelity, his honour. A right to know that if his heart wasn't hers it didn't belong anywhere else either.

He had always known that he owed his future Archduchess loyalty even if he wasn't lucky enough to offer her love and that was why in his few past relationships he had always been careful not to let his feelings grow beyond fond. To let his body and mind do the thinking, not his emotions.

He wasn't kidding himself that one kiss and a bit of flirting was enough to make Emilia fall in love with him. But neither could he kid himself that he wasn't falling for her. Hard. He was a rational, sensible man; he didn't believe in love at first sight. But the moment he had seen Emilia something in him had cracked. The way she had been lying under the tree, utterly absorbed in her work. The way she had responded to the garden he loved. The loneliness in her wary eyes. Her trust in him. The way she'd kissed him, fearlessly and sweetly. A kiss that should never be repeated. A kiss he would never forget.

For her he was probably a tryst at best and that was exactly as it should be. For him she was a glimpse of what his life could be like if he wasn't Prince Laurent d'Armaria, Archduke, absolute ruler and all that stood between his beloved country and bankruptcy.

So he allowed Emilia to take his hand and he vowed that he would treat her—and himself—to an evening neither would ever forget. And then he would let her walk away without a single reproach and he would get on with repairing his country.

Because that was what an Archduke should do.

The tunnel brought them out right at the foot of the cliff, onto a narrow ledge lashed by sea spray. There Laurent kept a small boat moored on a tiny jetty, sturdy and open, not robust enough to do anything but hug the rugged coastline, but still a taste of freedom found nowhere else in his narrow life except for those brief moments on his beloved bike.

'Your carriage, my lady,' he said as he pointed out the boat and her eyes narrowed.

'First a motorbike and now an open boat. Are you sure you're not trying to kill me?'

'The boat is completely safe.' He paused. 'You can swim, can't you?'

'I won't need to be able to swim if the boat is as safe as you say,' she pointed out and then relented. 'Yes. For a while I was in club training. As you can imagine, my mother hated it, all those five a.m. starts. I gave up after, well, when I went to live with my dad, but I'm still a strong swimmer.'

'Good. Sometimes I take the boat to deserted coves and swim. Maybe you could come with me one day.'

'That sounds lovely.' Emilia didn't point out that the chances of either of them having time to go swimming during the rest of her stay were slim at best and Laurent was relieved. Tonight he wanted to be like Ren, the man he had pretended to be when he'd first met Emilia, free of all ties and responsibilities, enjoying the company of a beautiful woman.

He helped Emilia into the boat and expertly steered it away from the rocks and along the shoreline, taking it further out as the cliffs gave way to harbours and beaches, the curve of San Tomare's famous promenade clearly visible with its waving palm trees and butter-yellow sand and elegant pastel-painted buildings, the mountains behind framing the picture-perfect whole.

Emilia said nothing during the boat ride but her eyes were wide as she took the scene in, her solemn mouth curved into a smile, showcasing her dimples. Fierce pride enveloped Laurent as he followed her gaze. San Tomare was the most cosmopolitan part of Armaria, but it was just one part of the country he loved; the mountains, the vineyards and olive groves, the alpine plains and the lowland rural grasslands, where the country's farmers still tilled and sowed as they had for hundreds of years, were just as important, just as impressive. But there was something special about the small capital city; no wonder tourists flocked here.

The city, the mountains, the plains, they were all in his keeping and he would do everything he could and all he should to ensure they prospered. But tonight… His eyes softened as his gaze moved to study Emilia, her straight hair whipped into a tangle by the sea breeze, her sallow cheeks pink with happiness, her eyes alight. He had never seen anyone or anything as beautiful as she was this evening, windblown in her jeans and jacket. He memorised every atom, knowing this memory would sustain him through the years to come.

Spotting the harbour, he steered the boat towards the long jetty he usually favoured, bringing the boat smoothly alongside with practised ease. Securing the boat onto one of the iron rings set into the jetty, he held his hand out to help Emilia from the boat. Her hand was cool and smooth in his, and yet he was aware of every millimetre of skin that touched his and he knew the feel of her hand in his would be imprinted on him for ever. How could a few hours change a man so profoundly? Maybe the Princess in *Roman Holiday* had a point—better a day of freedom than none at all.

'This is even more beautiful than the photos,' Emilia said, looking around as they started down the jetty, her eyes wide in appreciation, and Laurent was filled with a bittersweet happiness that he could show off the city he loved so passionately.

'A poet once said that San Tomare had all the history of Rome, the culture of Paris, the beauty of Vienna and the fierce pride of Tirana distilled into a few square miles of perfection.'

'I wouldn't want to contradict a poet,' Emilia said, her face glowing as they reached the end of the jetty, and Laurent couldn't help but remember Byron's immortal words: *She walks in beauty, like the night...*

'Come on then; let's see if you still agree after you've looked around.'

Laurent knew every inch of his city. Like all municipalities, San Tomare wasn't perfect. Some areas were far too expensive for locals, dominated by holiday lets and second homes, others needed investment, the inhabitants too often locked into a circle of poverty served by substandard infrastructure. If Clay Industries could be persuaded to invest here then all that could change, the opportunities for the youths and adults in the narrow streets transformed.

But this evening he would forget all his responsibilities and concentrate on all that the tourists flocked to San Tomare to enjoy, from the cobbled Italian quarter with its world-famous Roman amphitheatre to the celebrated beachfront promenade and the small but vibrant theatre district where Armaria's world-class ballet and opera companies were based.

At this time of the year the sun didn't set until late and they could wander through the soft pink evening light, Laurent pointing out the famous if slightly creepy puppet shops, stopping at a stand-up bar for bitter coffee followed by an eye-watering shot of the locally produced citrus liqueur sweetened with honey, and tiny plates of olives and cheese and tomato topped bread before they headed to the amphitheatre. Sometimes in summer the theatre companies staged plays or operas in the ancient space but tonight just a few tourists wandered around the circular stage, sitting on the stone seats or taking selfies against the dramatic backdrop. Laurent's heart swelled as he watched a young couple smiling into the camera, his arm protectively around her shoulders, the other angling the phone down as his girlfriend or wife snuggled in. What must it be like to be so carefree, to be able to choose where to bestow your heart?

But in the end did any of them have any choice at all?

'Come on,' Emilia said, tugging on his arm. 'Smile!'

To his surprise and slight alarm, Laurent saw her phone was in her hand, the camera switched on and toggled towards them. He always refused all requests for selfies and photos, wanting some little control over his life, to keep his inner self private. No wonder all his official photos and portraits were so stiff, like one of the puppets they had passed earlier, even the paparazzi shots showing a mannequin not a man. Was there a photo of him relaxed and smiling anywhere? Not that he was aware of.

His instinct was to pull away, but part of him wanted a memory of this evening's escape to be preserved on a cloud somewhere, for Emilia to come across it at some future date and remember the kiss they'd shared. So, instead of making his excuses, he smiled, leaned in so he could smell the sweet scent of her hair, so she fitted perfectly against him, and allowed her to take the picture.

'There you go,' she said, showing him the photo. 'Look at that backdrop.'

Laurent took the phone and stared down at the small screen and the two smiling faces. He barely recognised himself in the relaxed, laughing man, eyes glowing with happiness. 'Who is it that said that a photo captures a piece of someone's soul?'

'You've given me some of your soul then?' Emilia took her phone back and, although her tone was light, teasing, her eyes were full of questions.

'Yes,' Laurent said. 'And I gave it willingly.'

He'd told himself he wouldn't kiss her again, but how could he not when the sun was dropping below the horizon and the sky was purple and gold, when her face was full of hope and a tentative joy, when he knew it wasn't just part of his soul he had handed over this evening? She was still so close it was just a moment's work to turn to face her, to slip his arm around her slim waist and allow himself to savour the feeling of her skin under his touch, to imprint this moment firmly on his memories, to stare into the deep depths of her eyes and see her soul in turn and know he had been granted a rare and precious gift. One he would hold for just a few hours but remember for the rest of his life.

CHAPTER SEVEN

EMILIA COULDN'T BELIEVE this was her life. The whole evening was like a fairy tale. A dream. A soft-focus montage in a film.

It was like living someone else's life. Nights like this just did not happen to Emilia. She wasn't the kind of girl who got whisked off on a black steed—automatic horsepower rather than equine, but still—and kissed in a lemon grove and then again at the top of an amphitheatre as the sun set in a picture-perfect kaleidoscope sky. She had never before wandered hand in hand with a tall, handsome man through cobbled streets, stopping to kiss in doorways, before ending up in a tiny harbourside restaurant where flowers trailed from hanging baskets and violins played in the square beyond.

And yet here she was, champagne in hand,

a plate of fresh seafood in front of her, a candle separating her from said tall, handsome man who was looking at her as if she—mousy, reserved Emilia—was the most enticing, brilliant thing he had ever seen. If this was romance then she had been wrong to scoff at it for all these years. She just needed to remember that it couldn't be real. People didn't actually fall in love at first sight or in one evening, or even in one week. They fell in lust maybe, desire certainly, but the bubbles frothing through her veins, the sweet tension low down in her belly, the sheer physical awareness of every part of her body and how it fitted with Laurent's, that couldn't be love. It couldn't be that easy, that simple.

A week simply wasn't long enough to get to know someone properly. She was all too aware that you could spend months, years with a person and they could still reveal a part of them you had never guessed was possible, show an indifference worse than any deliberate cruelty. But she did know that Laurent was a good listener and somehow she could open up to him like no one else. That he knew all the most picturesque spots in the city. That he kissed like an angel—or maybe a devil.

Even if she was the kind of girl to change her life for a man, it simply wasn't possible. Laurent had obligations and ties she simply couldn't comprehend, whether Bella was part of his future or not. No, better to take this evening as exactly what it was, a perfect evening. A gift from a universe which had finally seen Emilia's aching heart and loneliness and decided to show her another way. A better way. She could take this confidence and knowledge back to England and try to expand her limited life.

'What would you like to do next?' Ren asked as the plates were cleared and the waitress poured the last of the champagne into their glasses. 'We could go dancing—ballroom, disco, country—there's a nightclub for any type you fancy. Or we could go to a late-night concert. Or we could just sit here and enjoy the view.' His gaze was fastened to her face as he said the last few words, not out at the moonlit sea, and Emilia's cheeks heated at the compliment—and at the desire clear in his eyes.

'They all sound appealing,' she said, picking up her glass and taking a too-large gulp of the tart champagne.

'Or,' Laurent said, his navy gaze intent on hers, 'we could head back to the villa. For a nightcap. See where the night takes us.'

'A nightcap?' Of course he'd suggested a nightcap. Wasn't that where evenings like this led? Walks and kisses and violins and champagne all led to nightcaps and then where? Her hand trembled as she held her glass, her smile less confident than she would like. But, for all her tell-tale nerves, she was tempted by the invitation, both spoken and in Laurent's eyes, the way his body leaned towards hers. She was sick and tired of regrets, of fear of rejection. And her body hummed with his proximity. Why deny herself?

This whole job was about moving on. Moving on professionally by getting the kind of publicity which would push the agency into another league, making enough money to give them security for the next few, crucial months. It was her apology to her father and his family and a farewell gesture to a childhood full of anger. Why not move on emotionally as well, start to think of creating a life full of memories she wanted to carry rather than memories that held her back? Move on physically, banish the shadows that haunted her and stopped her getting close to anyone.

She wanted to, every atom ached to. But actually taking the step would be a whole other leap and she just didn't know if she was strong enough.

'Or a coffee. If you prefer.'

'That sounds tempting.' It was Laurent who tempted her, not the nightcap. But she couldn't let things go any further, not while there was so much left unsaid. Walks and kisses were one thing. A nightcap or coffee and where they might lead quite another.

Laurent had no idea who she was, no idea she was related to the man he was putting so much work into attracting. No idea that the family she had told him about was the one he was considering marrying into. And even if she didn't tell him herself, he would find out soon enough. Her father, Simone and Bella were going to arrive in just a couple of days and she couldn't guarantee that her anonymity would be maintained. Better Laurent heard the news from her.

But what if the confidences she had so thoughtlessly shared made him confront her father and her dad didn't invest as a result? San Tomare was utterly charming, but Laurent had pointed out where it needed investment, jobs beyond tourism, farming and fishing, a reason for the university graduates to stay home rather than take their skills to France or Switzerland. Her father's company could be the first step in helping Laurent make the changes he needed. She would still be the selfish brat her father thought her if she got in the way of that.

And there was Bella. There was no love between the stepsisters, they weren't friends, spent no time together. But it wasn't Bella's fault. She had tried, back when they were children, and still made the occasional effort now. And she'd been in regular contact over the last two weeks, discussing costumes and dresses and asking for Emilia's opinion. Could Emilia really contemplate sleeping with the man her stepsister might marry? It seemed so sordid. In retrospect, all those cosy innocent picnics in the walled garden weren't half as innocent as they'd seemed. She was certain her family would not see them that way.

Twirling her glass, Emilia knew it was time to dissolve the spell and re-enter reality; she needed to find a way to tell him who she was. 'Can we walk?' she asked. 'By the sea?'

'Of course,' he said easily and if he was disappointed she had turned down the offer of a nightcap, he hid it. But then Laurent had plenty of practice at hiding his feelings. She just didn't want him to hide them with her.

It was a short stroll to the beach. The picturesque curve was lit up by the moon and the hundreds of fairy lights entwined around the palm trees fringing the road. Emilia inhaled the sea air and tasted salt on her lips. They passed a family as they headed to the shore, the parents holding hands while a small boy raced ahead and an older one walked by their side, exchanging greetings with a smile.

'Why has no one recognised you?' she asked, a question that had been hovering on the tip of her tongue all evening. 'You're on the bank notes, there's portraits of you everywhere and yet nobody has as much as done a double take.'

'You didn't recognise me when we first met,' he pointed out and she tilted her chin haughtily.

'I was new to the country and had yet to see a portrait or bank note. Besides, you looked most reprehensible. Who expects to see an Archduke in a dirty T-shirt and ripped jeans?'

'Exactly. Who expects to see an Archduke in casual clothes, taking a stroll with a girl in public? I learned a long time ago that the only way to have a private life is to do it publicly. The bike, the boat, the villa—no one expects me to own them and so they just don't see me. But if I was in my dress uniform with bodyguards then they'd know it was me. I like to hide in plain sight.'

'Very clever.'

'Very necessary. I don't get much time away from the castle, from Parliament and my duties, but just one bike ride, one night in the villa, one walk around the streets in a month reminds me of why I do what I do.'

'Did you ever question it? Ever think, *Sod it, I don't want to be an archduke and join the army and do a business degree. I want to ride my bike through Europe or be an artist. I want to marry whoever I want. Be whoever I want?* Did you ever rebel?'

Laurent was silent for so long Emilia feared she had overstepped. When he spoke at last his voice was quiet, pensive. 'The night my

father died he called me to him. He told me
that people would think that being an Archduke was fun, that having the power we still
have in Armaria gave us freedom. He told
me that those people were wrong. That my
inheritance was a great privilege and a great
responsibility. That Armaria was my destiny and I needed to treat the country and
my role with respect and honour. I have always tried to live up to his words, even when
they seemed like an unbearable burden. Even
when, yes, I wanted to take my bike and roar
off into the distance, although not to be an
artist. I'd soon have starved. But how could I
when my father laid this charge on me? Gave
Armaria into my keeping? I always knew my
destiny and tried to embrace it, not resent it.'

Emilia had promised herself no more
touching but she couldn't resist reaching
out and taking his hand. His fingers closed
around hers, reassuringly strong. 'What
would you be? If you weren't an Archduke?'

'No one has ever asked me that before.'
They walked a little longer while he thought.

'I always liked buildings. Maybe an architect, although the lack of drawing ability might be a problem. Or an engineer of some kind. How about you? Always wanted to organise events?'

Emilia was guiltily aware that she was supposed to be confessing who she really was but the evening was so warm, the sound of the sea lapping on the shore so beguiling, the conversation so easy, she put off the moment for a while longer. 'I fell into it really. When I left home I obviously needed a job and got one at a hotel, just as a chambermaid; I wasn't really qualified for anything. But the manager was really kind—and French. He liked it that I was half-French. So he trained me as a receptionist and then after another year I started to work in events at the hotel. A couple of years after that I went to work in conferences for a big corporate company and that's where I met Harriet, Amber and Alex. The rest is history. But it suits me. It's all-encompassing; when I plan an event I don't have the time or energy to think about anything else. And it's always a huge adrenaline ride. I'm at the centre of this whirlwind, you know? Everyone needs me and I control it all. It's terrifying and wonderful all at once.'

'Alex? One of your friends is male?'

She couldn't help smiling at the studied casualness in his voice. 'Short for Alexandra.'

'So who else is in your life? Any hopeful potential boyfriends sitting at home and checking their phones, wondering why you haven't texted this evening?'

She swallowed, looking down at their clasped hands. 'No.'

'Then English men are even more cold-blooded than their reputation,' he said.

'That's very kind of you.' She could barely speak, thanks to the lump in her throat.

'I'm not being kind; I'm being serious. What are they thinking?'

'I work all the time. I don't have time to date. And I haven't really wanted to.'

He stopped and she was forced to stop too. She still couldn't look at him. 'Ever? My every public move is followed by the world's media and I still managed to have several semi-meaningful relationships.'

'Did you love any of them?' she managed to ask, her throat still thick with fear and memory.

'No. I always knew that my marriage wasn't about me, it was about my country. Becoming an Archduchess—it's like you described running an event, standing in the middle of a whirlwind, trying to maintain control. It's not for everyone. Love seemed like a luxury. What if I fell for someone who didn't want to live such a life or couldn't cope with it? I didn't realise at the time, but I always kept something of myself back in those few relationships. And maybe that was a good thing. The girls I dated when I was younger found the public pressure far too much. If I'd loved them then imagine how hard that would be, knowing my country was the reason we couldn't be.'

'I fell in love once. At least, I thought it was love.' Was that her voice, so scratchy and raw? And what was she saying? No one knew this story. Not even her friends.

'But it wasn't?'

Emilia tried to loosen her hand from his grip but Laurent held on; instead she resumed walking and he kept pace beside her. 'No. It was infatuation on my side.'

'And on his?'

She'd asked herself that question a million times. 'Power, I think. It's an old story. Young, friendless girl meets older sophisticated guy and falls head over heels. Guy makes her feel like the most special thing in the world one minute and the most useless person alive the next. Girl never knows which guy she'll get, the romantic, loving one or the cold, critical one and she spends her life trying to please and appease him, desperate for his approval.'

'Oh, Emilia…'

She shook her head, not able to cope with sympathy. 'My attraction was my vulnerability. I see that now. I was like a puppy dog, just desperate for attention, for love. Willing to put up with anything for the pretence of it.'

'Did he hit you?' His voice was so cold it made her shiver.

'No. It never got that far. He moved on, thank goodness, bored of me and how pathetic I was. Found someone else desperate for his attention. But he made sure I knew he'd just been using me first. Made sure I knew just how easy I was, how useless. The words cut so deep because they were true. I tried to change my whole self to please him but, whatever I did, it was never enough. I just couldn't trust my own judgement after that. First my dad and then him. I put all my self-worth into their love and approval and when they withheld it I felt like nothing… It just seemed safer to be alone.'

'I don't want you to be alone.' His grip tightened on hers. 'You deserve so much more, Emilia.'

It was all too much. The confidences shared, the kisses, the whole evening. Emilia had worked so hard to keep her heart, herself, safe and she could feel her armour cracking and peeling off, her defences loosening. But there were things Laurent still didn't know and, whatever happened, only heartbreak awaited her. He was not free to love her and, even if he was, she wasn't exactly an Archduchess type, a former teenage tearaway with only one sordid relationship to her name.

All she knew was that she needed to feel something, do something. Breaking away from Laurent, she kicked off her trainers and waded into the warm sea waist-deep, her jeans instantly heavy and clinging.

'Emilia? What are you doing? Are you all right? Emilia!' Laurent called her name again but she kept going until the water reached her chest, soaking through to her bra, the sensation reminding her that she was still here. A survivor. She could survive this too, whatever this was. She turned at the sound of someone wading through water, only to step back as Laurent reached her.

'What are you doing? You're still dressed,'

she said foolishly and he looked at her incredulously before his mouth found hers in a kiss so deep and so full Emilia had no defences left, even if she had wanted them. She allowed him to pull her close to his cold, wet body, pressing even closer as if she could climb inside him, returning his kiss with a fierceness she didn't know she possessed, her arms sliding around his neck to pull him harder against her, mouth open to him, wanting all he was giving and more. Her breasts were crushed against his chest, her legs against his, and still she moved closer. She was dimly aware of a flash of light, of noise on the beach, but none of it mattered, only this kiss, this man, this moment.

When Laurent pulled away she couldn't help but mutter a moan of protest, her mind and body and lips aching for more contact. 'You're soaking,' he said ruefully and she laughed.

'Says you.'

He looked down at his dripping body almost in surprise. 'It's a good thing I have clothes back at the villa. Come on...'

Hand in hand, they waded out of the sea and weaved quickly through the promenading crowds enjoying the summer evening, slipping down side streets, Laurent pausing only to back her against a wall for another, fierce kiss.

Walking fast, they could have been back at the villa in less than fifteen minutes, but every few yards one or the other would stop to pull the other back into a desperate hot embrace. Laurent knew he should be cold in spite of the warm Mediterranean night, his clothes soaked through with sea water, but the spark between them didn't allow anything but heat. He'd never felt anything like it, this want. He couldn't fight it, not any longer. It was a sign that his life had to change. There was no way he could propose to anyone while feeling like this for another woman. And now his life had exploded into Technicolor he couldn't walk willingly into a monochrome future. He'd find a way to take care of Armaria and live the life he realised he craved. There must be a solution…

The villa gates swung open as he neared them, the door unlocked, not thanks to the sensor on his keys, wet through in his pocket, but his unseen bodyguards, and he cursed them as he shut the door firmly against the cameras and sightlines that invaded so many of his moments. But not this one. This was his alone. There were cameras in the house but not in his private suite, and he led Emilia up the stairs to the corner room with sea views and the large bed that dominated the high-ceilinged room.

'You better get out of those clothes,' he said, walking past her to the bathroom and grabbing a large towel. 'Here.'

Emilia leaned against the door and removed one boot and then the other, sliding her feet out of her socks with an almost balletic grace before shrugging her jacket off and unbuttoning her jeans. She made no move to take the towel he held out as she shimmied out of the tight, wet denim, pulling her shirt off in one fluid movement so she stood before him clad only in her still wet pink bra and pants.

'Your turn,' she said, her voice shaking despite the confident words, and Laurent knew he was undone.

He kicked off his wet shoes and socks, peeling off sodden trousers and shirt, dropping the towel as he did so. Emilia was staring at him, eyes wide, her sweet mouth slightly open, the heave of her breasts in the flimsy silk her only sign of life. Laurent was beyond thought as he drew her close, his touch both gentle and possessive. He was drowning in her, in her scent and her long smooth limbs and her touch. He skimmed his hands over her back, round to the dip of her waist, the swell of her hip, then back to the softness of her breast and heard her gasp as he did so.

'Laurent…'

She wanted *him*, not the Archduke, not the ancient name, not the castle. She wanted him and that thought was more intoxicating than any moment in his rigid dutiful life had ever been.

Their gazes snagged and held. 'Do you want me?' she whispered.

'More than I have ever wanted anything in my life.'

'That's all I need to know.' And, not taking her gaze away from his, she unhooked her bra and let it fall to the floor. 'And I think we've done enough talking for one night, don't you?'

Her words and gaze were bold but the wariness hadn't quite left her eyes—wariness and apprehension, maybe fear, as if she thought he might reject her. Reject her? It was laughable. She stood there, topless, her hair falling around her shoulders, emphasising the swell of her breasts. Laurent drank her in, unable to move. She was very slim, long-limbed, strong—a survivor, and he knew that her trust in him was a gift and not one she gave often or easily. 'You're so beautiful.'

'Tonight I feel beautiful. You make me feel beautiful,' she whispered and with that admission any thought, any vestige of hesitation was gone. All Laurent could do was take her into his arms once again, her skin smooth and warm against his, inflaming nerves he had thought dormant, turning his body into an explosion of touchpoints and sensation everywhere their bodies met. Chest, stomach, thighs, hands, mouths—he'd never been so overwhelmed before, never so lost in someone else's scent, their body, their whole being. As he scooped her up and carried her over to the bed Laurent vowed that this was just the beginning. That he would never hurt Emilia. They had met for a reason and he was never letting go. He'd find a way to make it work. He had to.

CHAPTER EIGHT

EMILIA STRETCHED IN the mid-morning light and glanced at the watch she always wore, a slim gold Swiss watch that had belonged to her mother. Gracious! She had overslept, and her desk wasn't a five-minute sprint down stairs and along corridors but several miles away…

And with that realisation the memory of the rest of last night came flooding back. The motorbike, the tour of the city, the meal, the way she had opened up as never before, the way she had trusted as never before. And the way she had felt as never before…

She wriggled, half in embarrassment, half in pleasure. Had she seduced Laurent or he her? Probably a little of both. She had never been so vocal, so demanding, so upfront about what—and who—she wanted before.

Closing her eyes, she relived the night, the touch and sensation, the gasps and exhortations to not stop, not yet, the low-voiced murmurs and laughter. She straightened, pulling the sheet up with her as she did so. How had this happened? How had she, Emilia Clayton, sensible and measured and always, always careful, fallen into bed with a man she hardly knew? A man who wasn't free to be there with her?

Maybe that was why. There was no future for them. She knew the ending before they started. How could she be hurt by him when he had never been hers? He was safe. Her heart should be safe.

But she had seen the way his eyes darkened when he told her she was beautiful. She had felt his soul when he kissed her. She would stake everything she had that he felt more for her than a fleeing attraction. But what he felt didn't matter. What she felt mattered less. Better to accept what was and move on. Let the night they had shared become a sweet memory. Their own *Roman Holiday.*

Sitting up, she looked around at the tidy, sparsely furnished room, all whitewashed walls and polished wood. There was no sign of either Laurent or his clothes, no sign that two of them had shared the bed, shared their bodies, were responsible for the rumpled sheets. Emilia rolled over and tried to block out the creeping negativity shivering through her despite her good intentions to approach her future with positivity, despite the look she had seen in Laurent's eyes, the way he had held her. Had she got it all horribly wrong? Misjudged everything? Trusted a man who was just after a night's fun before marriage put an end to his freedom? Had the connection she felt been nothing but a carefully planned seduction? Every instinct screamed no, but she had been so very wrong before. How could she trust her flawed instincts? Better to go on evidence, and the empty room spoke volumes.

She rolled back over, staring at the white-painted ceiling with its ornate plasterwork, and inhaled several deep calming breaths. Right, it wasn't as if she had slept with Laurent in the hope of a happy ever after. It was a one-night stand, no matter what his motivations. All she could do was control *her* thoughts and actions, no one else's. And right now her thoughts and actions needed to get her into the office, behind her desk and making sure every single detail for the ball was nailed down.

Mind made up, she slid out of the bed and padded to the bathroom, gathering up her clothes and bag as she went. Someone— Laurent—had picked them up from the floor where she had discarded them and hung them by the window so the sun had dried her damp jeans and top. He must have been up for some time. They were bone-dry.

The bathroom was as simple and elegant as the bedroom and the villa gardens. A quick shower and a face wash and Emilia felt ready to face the day, aided by a sweep of the deodorant and lipstick she always carried in her bag. Getting into yesterday's clothes wasn't too bad, although the jeans and jacket seemed too warm for what looked like another lovely hot day.

Returning to the bedroom, Emilia pulled her phone out of her bag, wanting to read her emails and anchor herself back in her world, but her battery had died in the night and her phone was unresponsive. Sighing, she returned it into her bag, knowing there was nothing else she could do to delay the inevitable and she was going to have to exit the bedroom and go in search of Laurent and a ride back to the palace. Wandering to the window, she looked out at the lemon trees in the garden and the sea beyond and was filled with a sudden intense urge to stay in this sheltered villa, in this moment. To be the girl who'd woken up in a rumpled bed, the sunlight slanting through the shutters, mouth swollen with kisses and a sweet ache deep inside for a while longer. But that girl was just an illusion. The real Emilia belonged at a desk with a phone in one hand

and a to-do list in the other. It was time she remembered that.

As she turned, stomach quaking at the thought of searching the house for Laurent, of finding the right words to say to him after her abandoned frankness last night, the door opened and he appeared, holding a tray. Emilia smiled, trying to hide her foolish relief. Of course he hadn't just abandoned her, wasn't regretting the night before. That wasn't how most people operated. But, she noted with a sense of foreboding, although he looked delectably morning-after-the-night-before, hair rumpled, chin and cheeks covered in morning stubble, his smile looked a little forced and wasn't reflected in his eyes, more grey than blue in the morning light.

'Morning, sleepyhead,' he said. 'I brought coffee; we don't have any tea. I hope it's all right.' He put the tray down on a small table near the other window; it was flanked by two armchairs. Her mouth watered; the tray was heaped with coffee, fresh fruit and delicious-looking pastries.

'Perfect. I usually have coffee in the morning,' Emilia reassured him. She hovered, unsure whether to kiss him or not, but he made no move towards her and so she stayed where she was. 'Do you have a phone charger? I really should check my emails. I had no idea it was so late.'

Laurent's smile dimmed. 'Yes, of course, but sit and have some coffee first.'

The sense of wrongness rolling around Emilia's stomach grew as she took the chair he indicated and accepted the cup of deliciously rich coffee he handed her, but shook her head as he offered her a pastry. 'I'm fine, thanks. Maybe some of that fruit first.' She paused, feeling foolish, but her instincts were screaming that something was wrong. He hadn't greeted her with a kiss or any kind of touch, his bearing formal and removed. 'Is there something wrong? It's okay,' she tried to joke. 'I'm not expecting a proposal. We both were carrying a lot of emotion last night.'

There was no answering smile. If anything,

Laurent looked more serious than he had before. 'Do you remember when I told you last night that I always had to keep a little part of me aside? That the demands of being my girlfriend often outweighed the benefits and that's why I stopped dating?'

'Yes, I remember.' She put down her cup, the faint foreboding that had shadowed her from the moment she realised she was alone intensified. 'What's going on?'

He didn't answer at first, pouring himself a black coffee and selecting a pastry he didn't eat, putting it down on his plate, crumbling it absently between his fingers. 'Very soon the Claytons arrive.'

'Yes.' Was this the *It's not you, it's me and my need to save my country* speech? He needn't worry. With all the hormones bombarding her last night she hadn't had an opportunity to tell Laurent the truth about who she was. When he found out she'd been less than honest she wouldn't blame him for walking away rather than nobly renouncing her. Maybe that kind of break was for the best rather than the *Roman Holiday—If things were different* type Laurent was heading for.

'I thought I knew exactly what I had to do. And what I wanted to do. Because no one was pushing me or forcing me. Wooing Bella Clayton was my decision. I need an heir, an Archduchess, and she ticked all the right boxes. I never expected more than compatibility in marriage and so how could I be disappointed when compatibility was my future?'

'Laurent, you don't have to explain. I knew what the deal was, what I was getting into. It's all right.'

He carried on as if she hadn't spoken. 'But then last night happened. Truth was, it didn't occur to me to factor something like you in, why would I? My world was so structured, so planned, random meetings and new acquaintances just didn't happen. But there you were, under my favourite tree. In my soul… You changed everything. You changed me.'

This was not how Emilia had expected

this conversation to go. 'Me?' she managed to say.

'Duty didn't seem too much of a burden when I didn't know anything different. But, although my mother knows what I was considering, although I am very sure Simone Clayton was also aware of my thoughts, I haven't committed myself to Bella, to anyone, not in any way. There, at least, I have nothing to reproach myself for. I promise you, Emilia. My heart was free for me to give where I chose.'

'I know all this,' she half whispered, both desperate and dreading finding out where this conversation was heading.

Putting his coffee cup down, Laurent straightened and looked directly at her, and with an effort Emilia met his gaze. 'Last night I made a decision. Duty is important, compatibility is essential. But love also has a place in marriage, even that of an Archduke. Bella is a very nice woman, but I don't love her and she doesn't love me. How can I ask her to share her life with me? How can

I pursue a relationship with her when I have spent the last week falling in love with someone else?'

'I...' This was so not how she had expected this conversation to go. They were supposed to agree that last night had been lovely, that it shouldn't have happened, return to the castle, and that would be that. Sure, it would have been difficult to watch Laurent with Bella but she had known the score before they started. She would have buried herself in work; it was always the remedy.

Now everything had changed and Laurent had said it was because of her. He had talked about love. Emilia's blood heated at the thought even as her mind recoiled in panic. 'Last night...' She shook her head, unable to stop her cheeks heating, to look directly at him. 'Last night was incredible. I've never felt like that before. Never imagined I would ever feel so...' She stopped again, not wanting to reveal so much, not even to Laurent, to whom she had already shown so much. 'But this is the next day and we're back to reality, Laurent.'

'The amazing thing about reality is that we get to shape it, if we want.' Laurent was watching her closely, so sure, so confident that this was right, and how she wanted to believe him. But she hadn't come here to fall in love. She wasn't prepared.

'Laurent, I don't know what to say,' she said almost desperately. 'To be honest, I didn't think that this was how this morning would go. It's not that I haven't started to develop feelings for you but we come from different worlds, different countries. Last night was supposed to be a one-off as a start; we both knew that. And that made sense. Apart from anything else, neither of us have time to start shaping reality. I have an incredibly busy few days ahead, you have guests to entertain.'

'Duty comes first?'

'I guess we have that in common.' She tried for a smile, needing to get away, to think. 'Look, I need to get to work. Can we meet and talk about this later? In the garden this evening?' The garden was their safe place. Maybe she could make sense of his words, of her heart, there.

'It's not quite that simple.' Laurent took his phone out of his pocket and slid it across the table. 'As you'll see.'

Emilia picked it up after a quick glance at Laurent, her mouth dry. As she tilted it towards her a picture flashed up, a wet-through Laurent kissing a brown-haired girl very thoroughly. Kissing her… 'The flashes of light,' she remembered, her heart sinking.

'Thumb through,' Laurent commanded and Emilia obeyed with shaking hands. Another shot of them kissing, one of them holding hands, heads tilted together, the desire on their faces so blatant Emilia gasped, feeling as exposed as if she had been naked.

Prince and Mystery Brunette! the headline read, followed by a breathless article detailing the Archduke's secret date and the mystery girl he hadn't been able to keep his eyes or hands off all night.

'Oh, my God.' Emilia set the phone back down, sickened. 'This is horrible. How can they publish these?'

'We were in public. I just didn't think. I thought we—I—hadn't been recognised. I often go out incognito, but I don't usually let my guard down to this extent.'

'I can't believe this is happening,' she whispered. Her father would see the photos, Bella would. Of course they would think she had sabotaged things on purpose. This ball was supposed to be her way of making amends and moving on, not building an even bigger wall between them.

'I'm sorry. I should have warned you this was a possibility. I thought we had covered our tracks, but I can never guarantee privacy. Do you regret last night?'

Emilia stared down at Laurent's phone, at the photo of her standing by the water's edge, her clothes wet through and clinging so that every part of her body was visible. She looked so vulnerable, every thought right there for anybody to see: hope, desire, need. How many people were looking at her right now? Sneering at her naked want, at her messy hair and see-through top. But then she looked up and saw a flicker of sadness in Laurent's otherwise perfect poker face. She wasn't alone here. Standing up, she walked over to Laurent's chair and lifted his head with her hands so he was looking directly at her.

'Neither of us know what's going to happen. We wouldn't if you weren't the Archduke, we wouldn't if those photos hadn't been taken. But one thing is certain. Last night was the best night of my life and if that's the one shot we get then that was a pretty good shot. You made me feel in a way I didn't know I could. You made me believe I was beautiful and desirable and I am so grateful—will always be grateful for that.' Emilia leaned down, her heart flipping as she inhaled his scent, sea and lemon and something uniquely masculine that was pure Laurent, pressing a gentle kiss on his mouth.

He didn't respond for a single surprised

second, but then he deepened the kiss, pulling her down so she was on his lap, his arms around her, kissing her greedily, desperately, as if he was trying to fit a lifetime in the one kiss. Emilia matched him, hungry kiss for hungry kiss, her arms entwined around his neck, fingers in his hair, pulling him closer until the shrill ring of his phone made them both jump and pull apart.

'I should get that…' he said and Emilia slid off his lap, trying not to touch her swollen lips as she did so.

'Yes. And then we had better get back. I'll wait downstairs.' And she was at the door before she could change her mind. She stopped as she reached it, turning back to look at Laurent. His eyes were fixed on her and she paused for a moment, allowing her heart to shine through her eyes, before turning and hurrying downstairs, feeling as if she had said goodbye before they had got much past hello.

Laurent walked heavily down the steps of the villa. It was so different to last night, pulling

Emilia up after him, breathless and thrumming with need and desire. Last night had been a beginning, this morning a kiss goodbye. They had barely got started.

It was easy, too easy, to blame the pictures. Nobody wanted to be photographed during their private moments, for the whole world to share what was meant to be intimate. But Emilia had begun to withdraw before then. She had withdrawn the second he had mentioned love.

He was a fool. He'd rushed into a huge declaration because of the photos, wanting her to know how he felt before she saw them. He'd forgotten how vulnerable she was, how damaged by her past. She needed wooing gently, not big gestures.

He could do that. It was almost a week until the ball. He had time. Of course first he needed to deal with the fallout of the pictures. The Claytons were due to arrive the day after tomorrow. He couldn't exactly apologise—that was the problem with unspoken understandings—nor did his carefully arranged programme for getting to know Bella Clayton better seem appropriate. But he could still entertain the family, showcase the best of Armaria and ensure that the Midsummer Ball was as magical as its reputation.

Clay Industries' investment didn't depend on an engagement, thank goodness. It had just seemed like a neat way to tie the family to Armaria, but all the reasons Mike Clayton had been interested in the first place were still valid. The sun, wind and tides, the educated, multilingual workforce, the rail, sea and air links... He just needed to sell those benefits as never before and hope Bella Clayton hadn't invested too much in the idea of becoming an Archduchess, for both the sake of the investment and also her own happiness. She wasn't in love with him, he knew that, but that didn't mean he wanted her humiliated. Thank goodness he had said and done nothing she or her family could reproach him with, and he was even more thankful she seemed far more interested in meeting Pomme and riding Armaria's famous bridle paths than spending time with him.

Emilia hadn't gone very far. She was curled up on the chaise in the hallway, scrolling through her phone—she must have found a charger somewhere. Her face was very pale, her eyes glassy and brow furrowed. Her tiredness didn't look like the result of a sleepless night, it looked like plain old exhaustion and all Laurent wanted to do was keep her here until her colour returned. In fact...

'Why don't you stay here for a few days?' he said, inspired. 'It's private, there's plenty of space. I could have a car take you anywhere you needed to go.'

'That sounds lovely, but I need to be on site.' She held out her phone towards him. 'Besides, there's something I need you to see.'

Laurent stepped over and took the phone, eyes creasing in disgust as he realised he was looking at yet another gossip site, another photo of a soaking-wet Emilia, her top almost transparent. 'Why are you looking at this? The best thing to do is ignore them; believe me, I know.'

'Read it,' she said.

After shooting her a troubled glance he quickly scanned the text.

Royally Yours *can exclusively reveal that the mystery brunette who indulged in a spot of late-night swimming with Europe's most eligible bachelor Laurent d'Armaria, Archduke and royal hottie, is none other than Emilia Clayton, who is in Armaria to organise the Midsummer Ball—which will also commemorate her father's sixtieth birthday.*

Emilia is the only biological daughter of tech king Mike Clayton, who has been rumoured to be looking at Armaria as a base for his newest factory.

Palace sources had hinted that Bella Clayton, Mike Clayton's socialite step-daughter, was in line to be the new Arch-

duchess. Was it all an elaborate bluff or has Emilia cut out her stepsister?

Either way, we can't wait to see what happens next.

Laurent read it again before looking over at Emilia, confused. 'I don't understand. How have they made such a mistake?'

'I was going to tell you last night...'

It took a moment for her words to sink in. 'It's true? The man who let you leave home when you were just a child? That's Mike Clayton?' Laurent just couldn't comprehend it, couldn't marry the serious but kind man he had met with the uncaring father Emilia had described, the close-knit family who had welcomed him into their home with the people who had excluded a hurt, grieving teen.

'Yes. At least...'

'Emilia, either it's true or it's not.' His chest tightened. How could he do business with such a man? But how could he not? He needed the Clayton millions—Armaria needed it.

'Everything I said was true,' she told him with quiet dignity, her chin high. 'My father had an affair, he left my mother and she was heartbroken. I didn't see much of him from the day he left until the death of my mother. He's not the only man to start a new family and see little of the old; it happens all the time. But that doesn't make it easier or right.'

'I know.'

'It's hard to explain, to put into words how angry I was, Laurent. Simone didn't want me but, to be fair to her, maybe she tried as much as she was able. She is so different to Maman, though. So calm and emotionless. I couldn't read her at all; I still can't. And Dad was so different when he was with her. It felt like a betrayal of all we had been, of Maman, of my whole life.'

'None of that excuses what they did.'

'No, it doesn't. And I don't excuse them, Laurent, but what I have realised as I've grown older is that there are always two sides to every story and their story would have some validity. I was very, very difficult. I already told you I used to stay out, truant from school, shoplift. I was also rude to Simone, always, not that she ever showed that she noticed, rude to Bella when I spoke to her. And when I say rude—' she shook her head '—sullen was a good day.'

'Emilia, I don't care how badly behaved you were. They were your family.'

'No, they weren't. That was the problem. It is the problem. They were—are—a family, and Dad and I should have been a family but we weren't; he belonged with them. The more I wanted him to show me that he loved me no matter what, the worse I got, the more he stepped back—I told you he had no emotional intelligence.' She paused, looking down at her phone, her eyes clouded.

'Maybe part of me thought if I was bad enough I could scare Simone and Bella away and then it would be just Dad and me and I'd get some part of my life back. Part of me just wanted them to hurt like I did. And I just wanted them to see me, to really see me, to acknowledge how I felt, to tell me it was okay. I wanted more from them than they could give, I think. It was like we spoke different languages and they just couldn't understand what I was begging for. I wish my father hadn't had an affair, I wish he had tried harder to see me after he left. I wish he'd shown me he wanted me and loved me. But in the end I was the one who walked out and I'm the one who stayed away. It was the only way I could protect myself. But when I look back I feel sorrow for how sad and lonely I was, but also shame for some of the things I said and did, and guilt for how much I tried to destroy his happiness. That's why, when Simone asked me to do the ball, I agreed. It was a chance to say I was sorry. A chance to show him who I am now, what I do. Maybe it still won't be enough, but I couldn't go on hiding away. I had to try.'

'But why didn't you tell me who you were?'

She tried for a smile. 'So many reasons. I couldn't work out if asking me to do the ball was Simone's way of keeping me in my place or an olive branch. I didn't know if

Dad would know I was involved, if I wanted him to know. All the publicity says that Dad has one daughter—and they don't mean me. It's so humiliating. Plus there were the rumours about Bella and you… It just seemed safer to stay anonymous. But I was going to tell you last night, until circumstances overcame us.'

'Right.' It wasn't often Laurent was at a loss but right now he didn't know what to say or to think. Emilia had been the most real thing to happen to him, but it looked like he didn't know her at all. He hadn't even known her name. Plus the already awkward situation with the Claytons had just taken on a whole new dimension. How was he going to explain to them why a member of their family had been plastered all over the tabloids, why their family was now in the gossip columns? He wouldn't blame them for taking their investment and walking straight out.

'There's a car outside to take you back to the castle. I'm afraid there's a lot of press around so it's not safe to use the bike. You go—there's something I have to sort out here.'

'Okay.' Emilia got to her feet, making no move to touch him as she left, as if the passionate kiss they had shared had never happened. 'I'm so sorry. I know I've ruined everything again, but I'll try and put it right. Goodbye, Laurent.'

Laurent watched her go, wanting to call her back, to tell her he didn't care who she was and what she had done. But he couldn't find the words, his mind still taken up with wondering how to unravel the mess he had somehow created, the deal to save his country looking more and more unlikely. He had to put Armaria first. His own heart would have to wait.

CHAPTER NINE

'YOUR HIGHNESS.' SIMONE CLAYTON swept into an elegant low curtsey, her daughter following suit, and with a laugh Laurent hoped didn't sound too forced he bade them rise.

'You are my honoured guests,' he told them as he led them from the helipad to the front of the castle with its imposing entrance. 'No formalities necessary. How was your journey? Let's get you settled; I believe your suite is ready. I hope Miss Clayton doesn't mind sharing a suite with her parents? You have your own bedroom and bathroom, of course. But we have so many people coming to the Midsummer Ball the castle is actually almost full.'

'Of course that will be fine,' Bella Clayton assured him, her smile seeming genuine if her gaze a little curious. She didn't seem at all put-out, to Laurent's relief. Her mother was cool, but then she usually was, and he recalled Emilia's words; she didn't show much emotion at all. Bella laughed. 'As long as the stable is expecting me and I get a chance to see the famous Armarian Spaniels then I am completely happy.'

'A suitable mare has been selected for you and the daughter of one of my aides has offered to show you some of the best rides around here. As for dogs, my own dog Pomme has recently fathered a litter. I'm looking forward to introducing you to the puppies and to the proud father, of course.'

'That sounds awesome; thank you so much.' Bella paused and touched his arm, her expression serious. 'I just want you to know I got my own costume. There's been so much silly stuff on all those gossip sites, and it just seemed best. I didn't want to fuel any more crazy talk by matching with you. I hope that doesn't put you out?'

'No, not at all. Very sensible.'

'Good.' She looked relieved. 'Where is

Emilia? I thought she'd be here? I wanted to chat about my new costume; she's good at things like that. The ones she found for us were great, so I wanted her input on this one.'

'I believe she's in her office; it's where she seems to be all the time. There's a lot to do.' Laurent was very aware of Mike and Simone Clayton's heavy stares at the mention of Emilia's name. A difficult conversation needed to be had—and soon. 'My mother is very much looking forward to meeting you,' he said, falling in next to Simone and escorting her up the grand stone steps at the front of the castle. 'She's arranged some excursions around the country—the joy of being so small is that everywhere can be reached in a day. I do hope you enjoy them.' If Simone Clayton realised what a huge honour having the dowager Archduchess as a tour guide was she didn't betray it by so much as the flicker of an eyelid. Laurent could see how her *froideur* must have been difficult for a hurting, lonely child to cope with.

He was still unsure how he felt about Emilia's revelations. Of course he had kept his identity from her at the beginning—who knew how long he might have continued to lie if the Contessa hadn't unwittingly outed him? He could hardly occupy the moral high ground. And he understood the awkwardness of the situation, why she would want to avoid speculation if people had realised who she was. But not to tell him? To sleep with him whilst keeping something so important concealed?

But, as she had said, she had meant to tell him that night, but instead it had swept them both away. It was unfair for him to blame her for that. Things had escalated so very quickly...escalated and then stopped and he hadn't seen her since. She hadn't appeared in the garden over the last couple of evenings and he hadn't wanted to fuel speculation by visiting her in her office.

But although he had hoped she would come to talk to him, even if it was for the last time, he hadn't been surprised when she didn't appear. He'd had the feeling she was saying goodbye before the revelation about her identity.

So here he was with her family and yet without her. It seemed wrong, but for the Claytons it had been this way for a decade. Emilia obviously believed she was as much to blame for the family estrangement as her father and his wife, and in some ways that seemed the worst thing of all. How could she think that a child had equal responsibility, no matter how badly behaved she had been? Laurent knew many people who had lost their way mid-teens, only to grow into fine adults. They had had firm, loving families to help steer them though. Emilia herself had grown into a responsible, hardworking, intelligent young woman, but that lack of stability had left deep scars.

That was all Emilia needed. Stability and unconditional love. And, much as Laurent longed to rush to her and promise her his heart, he held back. He had to fix the relationship with Clay Industries for his country's sake. Armaria came first; he knew it, Emilia knew it. And if that was the case then was he the right person to fix Emilia's bruised heart after all? Or should he step away and free her for someone who had no other ties? Who would always put her first. Would that be the right thing to do? It would be catastrophic if he got it wrong, let her down. Dishonourable.

For the first time in his life his head said one thing, his heart another. Maybe if he just saw her then things would fall into place.

They reached the top of the steps and the guards who stood on either side of the main doors, grand in their ornate uniforms, saluted smartly as Laurent ushered the Claytons into the castle hallway. The main doors led straight into a huge hallway, part of the original medieval keep, with thick stone walls covered with tapestries and huge wrought iron chandeliers suspended from the high ceilings. Corridors led off on three directions and wooden staircases on either side led to the gallery.

'This is the original part of the castle. It was modified and extended through the centuries and three hundred years ago turned into the structure we see today—but all those original parts are incorporated within the castle. This is the main ceremonial wing; the residential wing is to the left, the business wing to your right, and that includes the parliamentary chambers, and the domestic and administrative wing is at the back.' He frowned. 'I'm not sure if wing is the correct term when the building is a square?'

'Are the turrets original?' Bella asked and Laurent smiled.

'Sadly not. Most of the bits that look really medieval are eighteenth-century follies. Apart from this hall, which dates back to the twelfth century in parts.' So much history and he could trace his line right back to that twelfth century duke. Some Archdukes had managed peace, others had fought wars they might or might not have been responsible for. Some had built, others had plundered. His grandfather had tried to take a country ravaged by two World Wars in twenty years and give it stability, a goal his father had inherited. Their hopes rested on Laurent's shoulders now.

'Would you like to go to your rooms now or would you like some refreshments?' he asked. Both women elected to head to their suite to freshen up, but Mike Clayton asked for refreshments and Laurent led him to the library, ordering a coffee tray to be brought to them there.

'You are, of course, welcome on any of the excursions we have arranged for Mrs Clayton,' he said once the drinks had been brought in and the coffee poured. 'I have arranged some field trips for you as well; I hope that's acceptable. One to the sites that I thought might appeal to you if you did decide to locate your factory here and a visit to the university, and a tour of some of our transport facilities.' He paused, searching for the right words to say next. 'I owe you an apology. It can't have been pleasant seeing your daughter in the gossip columns. For me it's a way of life; I ignore them. But for the uninitiated it can be brutal. The speculation about your family must have been difficult.'

Mike Clayton added milk to his coffee before replying, his shrewd gaze fixed on Laurent as he did so. 'It hasn't been easy. We're not used to that sort of publicity. I thought it was Bella you were interested in. I wasn't aware you even knew Emilia. To be honest, I wasn't expecting to see her here. We're not close.'

'I believe your wife asked her to help plan the ball,' Laurent said and Mike Clayton nodded.

'So Simone said. It seemed a little risky to me; Emilia can be a little volatile. She takes after her mother. But apparently she's good at what she does. It will be nice to see her. It's been a while. Look, don't worry about those pictures. Emilia always had a knack of getting into trouble, of demanding attention. I'm just surprised this hasn't happened before.'

Laurent stared at the older man in disbelief.

'The Emilia I have come to know is steady and hardworking,' he said. 'And the only reason she was in that situation is because of me. I took her out without bodyguards and I'm the one the paparazzi are interested in. Believe me, your daughter has been nothing but professional since the day she got here.'

Not wanting the conversation to escalate, Laurent switched back to discussing the itinerary for the next few days until the coffee was finished and the two men moved onto the local brandy. Mike Clayton picked up his glass and swirled the amber liquid thoughtfully. 'I suppose you think I'm a terrible father?'

Laurent paused, torn between good manners, the knowledge that he needed to keep this man on side and his wish to tell Emilia's father exactly what he thought of him. 'Emilia said she wasn't an easy child,' he admitted. 'And from things she's mentioned it sounds like she wasn't. But she was very young. I lost my father when I was young, sir, so I don't know a lot about relationships between fathers and their children. But I hope mine would have stood by me no matter what.' He kept his voice polite but his expression was hard and fixed on the older man, who nodded as he absorbed the words.

'Her mother was a very emotional woman. She hated how much I worked, wanted a marriage of ups and downs, full of big dramatic gestures, whether that was breaking every glass in the house or some spontaneous romantic adventure. And for a while it was exciting, but then it was just exhausting. Simone was so calm; meeting her was like coming home after a storm. She was interested in my work, supportive… I could have handled the divorce better, but Marie made it hard, which was understandable but helped no one, let alone Emilia. I offered Marie the Kensington flat, but she refused and moved out to north London, blaming me for the upheaval. She didn't want me to see Emilia. She would cancel weekends or holidays, rearrange when we had plans…and when Emilia was with us it was clear she didn't want to be. Simone said we shouldn't give in, that it should be business as usual, but I wonder now if that was the right tack.' He downed the brandy. 'It's too late now.'

'Emilia said you didn't want to see her back then,' Laurent said slowly, unsure of how much of Emilia's confidences he could reveal. Mike Clayton nodded.

'To be fair to Marie, she believed her own dramas. I'm sure she thought it was true. She didn't even tell me she was ill; the first I knew of it was when the hospital called and we hadn't seen Emilia for months. I know,' he said, looking up at Laurent, 'that I have little excuse here. I'm just telling you how it was. The business was taking off so quickly I worked eighteen-hour days, seven days a week. And Emilia didn't want to be with us anyway. I assuaged my conscience by sending her things rather than trying to force her to see me. Then Marie was gone and Emilia blamed me for everything. The next four years were almost unbearable; she waged a constant war. When she left, we could breathe for the first time in years.'

'So you just let her go?' Laurent couldn't keep the blame from his voice.

'I arranged a job for her with an old friend of mine, a job that came with a room. I made sure she got the training she needed to move up, even though she'd not even taken her school exams. I paid off that unpleasant young man she took up with when she was eighteen, and I have put money aside for her every month. She could buy a house if she wanted to, invest it in that business of hers, but she doesn't want to know. She doesn't reply to my texts, never comes to the house. I know why, but I have no idea how we can start anew or if she would even consider it.'

'Does she know any of this?'

'I don't know,' Mike Clayton said heavily. 'I doubt it and now it's too late. But she looked happy with you. Once I'd got over the shock, it was nice to see her happy.'

Guilt stabbed at Laurent. She had looked happy in those pictures—he'd been so horrified on her behalf, at the invasion of her privacy, he hadn't taken the time to see beyond the headlines. And he'd made no attempt to see her since. He was no better than the man sitting before him. She deserved better than both of them.

'She was happy,' he said slowly before looking directly at the older man. 'Look, it's none of my business but I think you should talk to your daughter. Tell her what you told me. She needs to hear it and she'll only believe it if it comes from you. You owe her that.'

His bluntness might have just lost him a deal, but Laurent needed more than honour and duty. He needed integrity. And he needed to find Emilia.

The evening was drawing in, but Emilia barely noticed the pink streaks highlighting the sky; instead her gaze returned again and again to the archway that led into the courtyard. Of course Laurent might be too busy with his guests to come here tonight, or assume that she wouldn't be there herself after the two evenings she had missed. Or maybe he simply didn't want to see her, thanks to her lies.

Coming here was foolish; she knew that. But she needed to tell him goodbye before all the guests arrived and gossiped about them, before she had to keep a careful distance in public so as not to fuel that gossip. Goodbye and thank you. Tell him what his friendship had meant.

Closing her eyes, Emilia inhaled the now familiar scent of flowers and herbs. She had never been as drawn to a place as she had this garden. It had felt like home. But her home was back in Chelsea with her friends. A place where she could work and not think, where she was safe. Chest aching, she walked around the garden a couple of times listening to the evening birdsong until she heard footsteps in the courtyard and halted, her heart hammering in her chest. She pulled the key out of her pocket and held it with trembling hands until Laurent came through the archway. He stopped when he saw her, an incredulous smile curving his beautiful mouth, and she held up a hand to stop him coming closer.

'Hey,' she said.

'Hey.'

He looked tired, shadows purpling his blue eyes, his cheeks hollow, and her heart turned over at the sight. She wanted to hold him, to support him, but all she could do was stand there. 'How are my family?'

'Okay, I think. Bella adores the horse I picked out and she is in love with all the puppies. I suspect she'll be begging for one to take home. Remember I promised you a puppy too; you need to go and visit them.'

'Maybe later. Bella was raving about how sweet they are. I saw her yesterday. She's changed costume. She is now full-on Titania in white and silver robes.'

'Probably for the best,' he said and she nodded agreement, guilt coursing through her. Bella hadn't reproached her in any way, but her sister seemed instantly at home in

Armaria. In less than a day she had made friends and knew her way around the castle. She would have made a good Archduchess. If Emilia hadn't got in the way.

Her guilt recalled her reason for being here. 'I wanted to return this to you.' She held out her hand, loosening her clasp so that the key to the garden was clearly displayed. Laurent closed his eyes briefly and her heart ached at the hurt on his face.

'It's yours,' he said roughly. 'I had it cut for you. Use it, don't use it, leave it at the bottom of a drawer, do whatever you want, but it's yours.'

'Laurent…'

'Don't worry, Emilia, I get it. I understand. And I don't blame you. My world is intense. It's not for everyone. Those not born into it are wise to run away while they still can because, believe me, if we were to see each other again, those photos would have been just the start. You're doing the right thing.' She stepped back at the bitterness in his voice. 'You deserve better,' he added more gently.

'No, you deserve better,' she told him, clutching the key so tightly it cut into her hand.

'I wish things were different, Emilia. I wish I was Ren, that my life was uncomplicated and free, that I could take you out and no one would notice us. That I could woo you and we could fall in love slowly and sweetly. But that's not who I am. I come with all this...' He made an expansive gesture, taking in the castle. 'I come with press intrusion and all-night policy sessions and pomp and ceremony. And it's exhausting. Whoever marries me marries all this as well. It's not easy. But I'd be there, supporting them every step of the way. Supporting you. If you would stay here a little longer. Let us get to know each other properly. See if this is real or not.'

She squeezed the key harder until her hand whitened around it, welcoming the discomfort. His offer was so tempting and who knew? Maybe back at the villa she might have agreed. But she'd had a lot of time to think since then. A lot of time when he hadn't called and she'd remembered how much relying on someone else for your happiness could backfire. A lot of time to remember how much worse it was to love and lose than just keeping yourself away from anyone who could hurt you.

'What about my dad? About Clay Industries?'

'I don't know. He's agreed to the itinerary I prepared. It's a start. But I think he loves you, Emilia, in his own way.'

'Don't,' she whispered, holding up her hand again, needing him to stop. 'I can't hope, Laurent, because it will tear me apart to lose him again. Maybe I'm a coward because I can't take a chance on him or on you. One day you'll realise that I'm no one special and I won't be able to take it. So this has to end now. While I can walk away with my head high and memories to light up the darkest days. Please understand.'

'You are special,' he said roughly. 'Why can't you see that? Why can't you believe in yourself the way I believe in you?'

'Everyone leaves me, Laurent.' She was willing herself not to cry, willing the tears to stay in her throat and her chest and the heat of her eyes. 'Please don't ask me to try.' She knew she was probably passing up the greatest chance of happiness she would ever be offered, but she didn't know how to grab it. Didn't know how to risk it all.

'I'll tell you what's real. How about the ball you have put together with love and care and attention especially for a father you love despite everything? What about the friends you talk about all the time? The business you're building up? You can love and be loved, Emilia; I see it in everything you do. Won't you let me try to show you?'

His words were intoxicating but she couldn't let them go to her head. 'Your friendship has changed me, Laurent. I know I must look pathetic to you, but it has. The evening I spent with you was the most romantic eve-

ning of my life, the night we spent together...'
She paused, cheeks hot with memory. 'That
night... I never thought it could be like that,
that I could *feel* like that. I've spent my life
trying to mean something, to be someone,
working harder and harder looking for approval, to be needed, and in one night I finally felt whole. Like I mattered. And it was
the most wonderful gift I could ever have
had. I will never forget it and never forget
you.'

'But you won't stay?' The disbelief in his
voice almost undid her but she had to stay
firm.

'You need a proper Archduchess, someone
brave and strong.'

'I need you,' he said but she shook her
head.

'I can't, Laurent.'

He looked as if he were about to say something; instead he paced up and down the
path for a moment before coming to a halt
in front of her. 'You deserve so much more
than you'll allow yourself. And it's out there

for you, Emilia. Please don't be afraid to try. Don't be afraid to reach for what you want.'

Emilia stared at him, tears clouding her vision. 'I…'

'Promise me,' he said, taking her hand. 'Promise me you won't hold back. I can't guarantee you that everything will work out. I can't promise you a happy ever after and that everyone you want will stay with you. But I can promise you that life is so much more worthwhile if you live it. I realise that now. I know it, thanks to you. It might be safer to live life with no ups and downs but if you do, Emilia, you will never get to enjoy the view. I'd like to think that one day you'll allow yourself to enjoy the view, even if I'm not standing next to you. And promise me that you'll remember that I tried. That I love you. That I saw you.'

She could hear no more. Emilia's mouth trembled as she extracted her hand from his. Standing on her tiptoes she pressed one brief kiss onto his cheek. 'I'll try,' she promised.

And with that she turned and was gone. It wasn't until the gate closed behind her that she realised the key was still in her hand.

CHAPTER TEN

LUCKILY FOR EMILIA the work piled up so high that even she began to feel overwhelmed, six hours' sleep dwindling to five and then four, and yet her to-do lists got longer and the amount of unread emails lengthened. But she was glad. Her workload meant she didn't have time to wonder if she'd made a huge mistake—and it gave her a legitimate reason to steer clear of her family.

All she had ever wanted was someone to really see her, to want her. Yet, instead of embracing it—and him—she was walking away without a fight. Was she walking away because she felt that Laurent was genuinely better off without her, that she was the wrong person to be an Archduchess, or was it because she was scared? Probably both, but whatever the answer she felt constantly empty, a gnawing pain in her chest and stomach.

Was she being incredibly brave or actually a coward, giving up far too easily, keeping their relationship as one perfect night, a dream that would never be sullied by reality?

Emilia huffed out a sigh, rubbing her temples as she did so. She didn't have time to keep turning the situation around and around. Not every guest wanted to dress up and follow a theme so she had ended up buying several hundred cloaks and masks for guests to use and discard after the midnight midsummer celebrations and needed somewhere to display them near the entrance. She had also needed to rethink some of the decorations and reorder the order of the music, her father's favourite band being more rock than classical, a strictly after midnight affair. Not that she minded being busy. Better too much to do and no time to think than actual time to sit, brood and mourn.

Thank goodness the ball was tomorrow and she would be home by the end of the week. Home to lick her wounds, regather her thoughts and whatever other clichés would help her get through this mourning period.

She opened up her email, wincing at the sheer number to have invaded her inbox in the last couple of hours, when her door swung open with a bang.

'I don't know, this isn't as bad as you claimed. Sure, there's no natural light, and the stone does rather scream ex-dungeon, but you've got a potted plant so it's all looking good to me.'

'Alex?' Was she dreaming? But no, there was her friend and business partner, as tall and effortlessly elegant as ever in a wafty maxi-dress which would make Emilia feel as if she were wearing a sack but on Alex looked like the cutting edge of fashion. Her hair was swept up into a chignon, her make-up perfect. Of course it was; Alex always looked perfect. 'What are you doing here?'

Alexandra didn't answer; instead she placed a tablet on the desk in front of Emilia. The screen wavered for a moment and then came to life to show two smiling faces; her heart swelled as she saw Harriet and Amber.

'Hi, Em,' Amber said.

Harriet chimed in with, 'Emilia! How are you?' at the same time.

'Radio silence, Em, not cool at all.' Amber shook her head reproachfully.

'I haven't been silent. I have emailed you approximately one hundred times a day.'

'You haven't spoken to any of us since those photos were published.' Harriet's brow creased with concern. 'We need to know you're okay.'

'Come on,' Emilia tried to joke. 'Which of us hasn't been photographed in a compromising position with an Archduke and had the pictures sent around the world?' But her joke fell flat.

'Are you two together? Does Simone know? I'd love to see her face when you sweep into the ball on his arm and she has to curtsey to you!' Amber's green eyes gleamed. 'I want an enlarged photo to hang on my wall.'

'It'll have to be Photoshopped as it won't

happen. There's no together, Amber. Sorry to puncture your romantic dreams.' Emilia hadn't meant to sound so curt and she tried to force a smile. 'Look, I didn't realise Laurent was who he is when we met. I thought he was a handyman or a gardener or something.'

'He lied to you?'

'Way to go, Em!'

Her friends' contrasting reactions made Alex and Emilia exchange smiles.

'Do we need to kick his ass?' Alex asked. 'Archduke or not, no one gets away with messing my friends around.'

'No ass-kicking required. We parted by mutual consent.' That wasn't exactly true, but if she admitted that he'd asked her to try and she'd walked away her friends would be horrified. 'He has a country to put first, and you have to admit I'm not Archduchess material.'

'You could be anything you wanted to be,' Amber said loyally.

'No, lust and liking isn't enough, not for

someone like Laurent. People like him marry for security, money, power. And who's to say that those marriages aren't successful? At least you both know exactly where you stand and what you want.' Say it enough and she might believe it. Forget the hurt in his eyes when he'd realised she wasn't going to even try.

'And how do you feel about this?' Harriet asked.

Emilia grimaced. 'My feelings don't matter, Harry. I'm not here for romance. I'm here to do a job, and that's what matters.'

'You like him though, don't you?' Alex asked, her dark-eyed gaze unreadable.

'Yes,' Emilia admitted. 'I do.'

'Do you love him?' Amber asked.

'I barely know him, Amber!'

'That's not what those photos looked like.' Amber's grin was gleeful. 'I'd say you know him rather well indeed.'

'I like him, I fancy him, I respect him. Are you satisfied? But love? I don't know what love is, I've never been in love, not the real thing. I think it might have been possible, in another world, another situation, one day. But I'll never know; it's just a might-have-been. Something short and sweet.'

'I think the lady protests too much,' Amber yelled as Harriet dug her in the ribs. 'Ouch! Harriet!'

Harriet ignored her. 'You didn't answer, Em. How do you feel? This whole situation is messed up. Your dad is there, along with your stepmother and Bella and now there's this whole situation with Laurent. That's a lot for anyone. So don't tell me you're fine. Tell me how you feel.'

Emilia made a point of sighing loudly but no one responded. Alex folded her arms and leaned against the office wall as if she had all the time in the world and Amber and Harriet stayed so still they seemed more like a screenshot than living, breathing women.

'I don't know, okay?' Emilia said finally. 'I don't know how I feel about any of it and I think it's better that way, better not to think or feel, because that way I can get up every day and arrange a party for the father who replaced me with a new family, and pretend not to hear people talking about me while I do my job and be brave and say goodbye to a man who might be my only chance at happiness. The man I think I might have loved tells me he thinks he might be falling in love with me and yet I let him go because I'm too scared to trust in him. And he's a good man, an amazing man, and he respects my feelings and that should make me happy, but actually I want someone to fight for *me*. I want Laurent to fight for me, even though I told him goodbye. I want someone to think I'm worth everything. I'm so tired of being replaceable...' She stopped with a gasp, aware that her voice had got louder and louder, that her eyes were hot with tears, her throat ached. She couldn't give in now. She couldn't feel, not properly, because if she did she wouldn't be able to carry on.

'Oh, Em,' Harriet said softly.

'I'm...'

'You're not fine,' Alex said firmly. 'And

that's okay, Emilia. We don't need to be fine all the time and it's not weakness to let our friends take care of us.'

Emilia didn't point out that Alex never let anyone take care of her, that she kept herself hidden away behind her cool façade. She knew why the other two had no family, why their friendship was so important to them. Harriet had lost her mother at a young age too, something the two girls had bonded over, and she had spent her teens and early twenties caring for her father until his dementia advanced to a stage where she couldn't manage any more. Harriet had been the loneliest person Emilia had ever met—except when she looked in the mirror—but since her engagement she had transformed into a lighter, brighter version of herself. Amber had walked away from a family who had wanted her to live in a way they approved of, shaking off their rigid constrictions for freedom and a life she chose for herself. It was a brave choice and Emilia could only applaud her friend for her unfailing optimism and belief that happiness awaited her. But Alex? None of them knew why she had been alone the Christmas Eve they'd first met and every Christmas after that, why she'd shared her inheritance with them, giving them both a home and business premises, who her family was and why she was estranged. They didn't know and they never asked. There was a wall around Alex even they couldn't push through.

'I don't need taking care of,' she said instead. 'I appreciate you coming here, Alex, but it's unnecessary. I just need to keep working.'

'I'm here to do the PR,' Alex said coolly. 'The guest list, the castle, the entertainment all is very tabloid friendly—even without the Archduke's much photographed amorous encounter. I offered our services to the castle press office and they agreed to let me come over and handle it as you're here anyway. I get the impression they usually find it much easier to control the story; this ball and the speculation around it is out of their league.'

'But while she's there,' Harriet said, 'she can make sure Amber and I are in the loop so we can manage any other issues from here, and that means you, Emilia, my dear, are free to go to your father's ball.'

Panic seized her chest. 'No. Impossible. I don't have a dress.'

'I brought one with me for you,' Alex said.

'It needs to be a costume...'

Alex didn't bother replying but her look said it all. Of course she'd bought a costume—and shoes and evening bag and jewellery and anything else Emilia might need.

'And I have a whole timetable to oversee—there are eight different bands in three locations, a formal sit-down dinner, a buffet, chocolate fountains, cheese buffet, canapés and an ice cream truck. There are acrobats and ballet dancers and a magician, a children's choir and a troupe of Shakespearian actors. There's a candlelit procession, country dancing and a midsummer celebration at midnight. Champagne bar, gin bar, craft ale bar and a speakeasy in a marquee outside, complete with cabaret. To say nothing of approximately five hundred guests arriving today and tomorrow.'

'Five hundred guests whose accommodation has been organised, transport from the train station or airport sorted, and coaches to and from the castle booked, each one with a steward to look after any mishap?'

'Well, yes, but...'

'And the castle housekeepers and stewards all have copies of this timetable?' Amber said, waving the carefully updated and very lengthy event plan that had been Emilia's bible over the last few weeks.

'Yes, but...'

'We can manage from here. And you've got your watch.' Emilia had a very expensive smartwatch that looked like an evening watch but received messages and allowed her to send them, which she often used when carrying her phone around was impractical. 'We can contact you if we need you.'

'And I'm right here,' Alex reminded her.

'But I'm not invited.' And that was the

crux of the matter. She wouldn't push into an event she wasn't part of, into the family that didn't need her. Watch a man she knew so intimately dance with other women and smile as if her heart wasn't breaking. As if she hadn't walked away from a chance of real happiness.

'You're the guest of honour's daughter,' Alex said.

'And you could dance with Laurent,' Amber said softly, but Emilia shook her head.

'No. I shouldn't. I bet Gregory Peck didn't follow Princess Ann around like a constant reminder of what might have been.' Three blank faces greeted this pronouncement and Emilia vowed to make them all sit down and watch *Roman Holiday* once she was back.

'Em, don't turn this opportunity down. Don't look back with regrets,' Harriet said. 'I know it's not easy, just be there to wish your dad Happy Birthday.' Her smile was wistful and Emilia knew that her friend was thinking of her own father, now living permanently in a past where Harriet didn't exist.

'Okay.' Much as she hated to admit it, her friends were right. She didn't want to watch her father's birthday from the sidelines, not again. And the costume element gave her the advantage of a disguise. She could take the opportunity to wish her father a happy birthday—and then make sure she disappeared before Laurent knew she was there. 'I'll put the dress on and I'll go for a bit, if you promise five-minute updates and to let me know immediately if anything isn't perfect so I can fix it. I will not have Simone finding fault with a single thing.'

'Deal.' Alex smiled as if she had no doubt that this was where they would end up. 'Let Amber and Harriet take care of all those last-minute details I can see you fretting over and I'll show you the dress I brought. It should fit, but better to find out if it needs altering now rather than tomorrow. And then you can show me this beautiful castle and the city and let me know everything I am going to need to run this event and any potential PR stories, positive and negative. I'd rather have all the responses drafted out in advance. This event is really going to put the agency on the map. I need to make sure we get the recognition we need.'

It was the calm before the storm. After all the painting and re-plastering and buffing, all the threading of fairy lights and erecting of marquees and stages. After weeks of frantic preparation the castle was ready, humming with anticipation. Laurent strolled through the beautifully decorated ballroom, admiring the flowers which brought the midsummer theme inside, the beautiful table decorations and all the love and care bestowed on the event. Emilia's hand was everywhere.

She'd be at the ball tonight; he'd made sure of it, contacting her friends and asking them to stage an intervention. She deserved to enjoy all her hard work. The big question he had yet to answer was whether he would respect her decision to say goodbye or fight for the woman he knew he loved.

He wanted to swoop in with an answer for

every objection and show her he was there for her no matter what. But he also knew how scarred she was, how frightened. She needed to be shown respect, to know that he understood her and listened to her. Somehow he had to find the line between respecting her and giving her the reassurance he knew she wanted. It was a fine line and he had to tread more carefully than he ever had before. He still wasn't sure what to do. He just knew he couldn't let her leave without trying one last time.

The alcoves had been disguised with gossamer curtains ready for dancers to sit and cool down or couples to slip away from the crowd and Laurent sat down inside one, enjoying the momentary peace. He had spent the last few days being the most gracious host he could, selling Armaria as subtly but clearly as possible. He could do no more. The only misstep had been the moment he'd showed Mike Clayton exactly what he thought of the way he'd treated Emilia and he wouldn't change that moment even if he could. Not even for the guaranteed investment.

Lost in thought, he didn't realise anyone else was in the room until he heard voices. A familiar voice that haunted his dreams.

'Dad? What are you doing here? You should be getting ready. Happy Birthday, by the way.'

'Thank you,' Mike Clayton replied. Laurent looked around for a way out of the alcove without being seen but there was none. He froze. If he left now would he interrupt the conversation, maybe kill it before it got going? But eavesdropping was dishonourable.

He sat back. Maybe it was dishonourable to stay, but he'd learned this week that sometimes honour wasn't the most important thing. Emilia needed to have a conversation with her dad; nothing should get in the way, especially not him. He grabbed his phone and tried to distract himself with emails, but the curtain was thin and their voices clear.

'It all looks amazing, Emilia; you've worked very hard.'

'Well…' he could hear the smile in her voice '… Simone pays well. Besides, I owed you about a decade worth of birthday presents and I did make a fool of myself at your fiftieth.' There was a long pause and when she spoke again she was barely audible. 'I should never have said what I said. Or thrown that drink.'

Thrown a drink? Well, she said she'd been a teenage tearaway and, knowing her history, Laurent didn't altogether blame her.

'We never meant to make you feel like we didn't want you, Emilia. I hope you know that.'

'Part of me does. I'm sorry about the photos too, Dad; they were embarrassing for all of us. I hope Bella wasn't too disappointed. Or you. I know you hoped that she and Laurent…'

'That she and Laurent?'

'That she became an Archduchess.'

There was a startled pause before Mike

Clayton laughed. 'I'm not denying that Simone probably fancied being the mother-in-law of an Archduke but you know Bella; she was far more excited about seeing the puppies than she was about seeing Laurent again. No, when she settles down it will be in a large country house full of animals and kids and the kind of chaos that makes Simone shudder. She's made to be a farmer's wife, Bella, not an Archduchess. What about you? The two of you seemed…' he paused awkwardly '…close.'

'Oh, Dad, can you see me as an Archduchess?'

'Once no, but we all grow up, Emilia. And you've grown up into a fine young woman. Your mother would be very proud. That agency of yours is well thought of, you're good at what you do, people admire you. I don't see why not. If that's what you want.'

'You think Maman would be proud?'

'How could she not be? I am, Emilia. What you have achieved here is amazing.'

'You are?' Through the curtains Laurent

saw the outlines of two people embracing and his heart nearly burst at the realisation that Emilia was finally getting the affection she craved from her dad. He glared at his phone as he concentrated on his messages with every bit of willpower he had, managing to give the pair the privacy they deserved until the sound of his name distracted him.

'He seems like a nice young man, your Laurent.'

'He's not mine.' Yes, he vowed, he was. 'Have you had a good visit?'

'It's an interesting country all right.'

'Interesting enough to build your factory here? Oh, Dad, please consider it. I know you want renewable energy and the conditions are perfect; Armaria is already much further along than most countries. The links are perfect, sea, air, rail, road and river, the education system is good. And Laurent is an amazing Archduke. He really cares, Dad, wants Armaria to be the best it can be, for the people here to have every opportunity. He'd work with you to make sure you had everything you needed, I know he would. You couldn't do better.'

'You're quite the ambassador.'

'I've been here for just three weeks and it feels like home. I can't help but care about what happens here, even after I leave.'

'Well, just between us, I am very close to making a decision. I was very impressed with that Laurent of yours. He isn't afraid to stand up for what he thinks is right and I respect that. I'd better go—we have a formal dinner before the ball and Simone will want me to start getting ready. Save your dad a dance tonight.'

'I will.'

'And Emilia? I'm glad you're here. Let's do better. Both of us.'

Laurent stayed still until he was sure both Claytons had left, his mind whirling. Not only had Mike Clayton practically assured Emilia that he was going to build his factory here in Armaria, but he had told Emilia he was proud of her. The words he knew she'd needed to hear.

Not only that but it seemed as if Laurent's intervention had been the right thing to do. Here it was, proof that seizing the moment was as important as planning. Emilia would be at the ball tonight. He had one last chance to convince her to trust in him and their relationship, one last chance to show her she was worthy of love. He could plan—or he could look for the right moment and seize it.

He'd been too cautious earlier, talking about getting to know each other better, thinking she needed slow and gentle wooing, allowing her self-doubt to push him away, aware as he was of all the problems being with him could entail. And those problems existed, but surely together they were strong enough to cope. Maybe he needed to go all in, show her just what she meant to him.

Mike Clayton was right—she had been a brilliant ambassador for Armaria, and she would make a brilliant Archduchess if she just believed in herself. In him. He'd known her the moment he'd laid eyes on her, fallen a little harder every stolen evening they'd spent together. He could live without her, but he didn't want to. Now he just had to convince her that he loved her, and find out if she loved him enough to try.

CHAPTER ELEVEN

'I LOOK RIDICULOUS.' Emilia stared at herself in the mirror and just about managed not to laugh. 'How on earth did you get this dress here, Alex? There's no way it would fit in a suitcase.'

'You look perfect,' Alex assured her. 'Very in keeping with the theme.'

'It's not very practical, not when I might have to come and help out at any moment.' She smoothed down the fabric of the dress. It was ridiculous but she couldn't help but admit that it was actually very pretty too. If she was five it might be the perfect dress… It was strapless and tight fitting around her bust and waist, before flaring out into a very full skirt. It ended mid-calf level at the front, curving to a small train at the back. The creamy buttery yellow looked warm against her sallow skin, the whole embroidered with shots of silver thread so the dress sparkled as it caught the light. A pair of silver shoes fitted perfectly, the heels surprisingly comfortable, her only jewellery a pair of sparkling statement earrings. Her hair was piled up into a chic knot, a mask, also silver, covering just her eyes.

'There is no need for you to come and help. Everything is under control. The masks and cloaks are being handed out as guests arrive to those that need them, all the food is ready, the musicians are here, the entertainers are warming up and the formal dinner is nearly over.' Alex shot her a hard stare as she spoke. She'd tried to persuade Emilia to go along to the dinner, but Emilia hadn't been able to face the idea of the other guests watching her and Laurent. Besides, for all Alex was willing to help, there were a hundred and one last-minute things that only Emilia could check.

But she had been fine not going because she had had the first real conversation with her father in two decades. A conversation in which he had told her he was proud of her. A conversation in which she had persuaded him that Armaria was the right place for him.

It had been easy to do. She hadn't realised until that moment how much she loved the country. Partly because of its charm and partly because it meant so much to Laurent.

Laurent. Her stomach tumbled. Had she done the right thing? How could she think so when knowing her stay was nearly over and she might not see him again felt like the end of the world?

'I think we're ready,' Emilia said, the nervous knot in her stomach partly the adrenaline that any large event always produced, especially one put together on such short notice, and partly nerves at the evening ahead. 'But call…'

'Call you if I need you. I know. I got it the first ten times.' But Alex smiled as she spoke. 'So what's your plan?'

Emilia inhaled to calm her churning nerves.

'I'm going to find my dad and say Happy Birthday and give him my present, have the promised dance. Not pour a drink over him, so already we're doing a lot better.'

'And Laurent?'

'I…'

'Look, Emilia. I understand, I do. Of course you want him to fight for you; that's completely understandable. But sometimes we have to fight for ourselves. If all that's standing between you and him is your fear then the only person who can really overcome it is you. It's your battle. He can't win this one for you.'

'I…' She stared at herself in the mirror, almost unrecognisable in the beautiful dress, her skin olive from the Armarian sun, her hair naturally highlighted, her eyes bright. 'You make it sound so easy.'

'Oh, Em. It's not easy. That protective shell has kept you safe. Telling Laurent how you feel about him, letting him convince you to believe in him, is going to take a huge amount of courage. But I know you have that courage,' Alex walked around Emilia, pulling the dress into shape.

'Do I? Sometimes I think I do, but then it all seems too much.'

'We've been friends for—what?—three years? In all that time you have never put yourself out there, Em. You've kept your heart hidden. Look,' she added quickly, 'I know—pot, kettle and all that. But I'm not the one about to go to a ball where the man I love will be and hide from him all evening because that's safer than being honest with myself, safer than being vulnerable—you are. Do you really want to come home with me, knowing you didn't even try to talk to him? To tell him what you told us? To tell him you love him.'

All Emilia could do was stand and gape. Alex's words were so close to her own thoughts it was uncanny—and painful to hear them spoken out loud.

'I don't know what to do, Alex.' She could barely get the words out, her voice small, the admission of failure difficult to say and acknowledge.

'You love Laurent?'

'I do. I love him.' Saying the words so plainly shocked her; the lightness in her heart as she said them was even more of a shock. She turned her bewildered gaze onto her friend. 'I do,' she repeated. 'How is that possible? After so short a time? Maybe I'm mistaking lust for love? Because I certainly feel that too...'

'I know,' Alex said. 'I saw the pictures.'

'But it's more. I love how he cares for this whole country, every person in it. How I can talk to him and he seems to understand when I barely understand myself. And I love the way he makes me feel, like I'm precious and special...'

'Don't tell me,' Alex said. 'You need to tell him.'

'But what if he changes his mind, or I mess up...?'

'No, no more excuses. Tell him. What's the worst that will happen?'

Emilia's stomach lurched. 'He'll laugh. Or he'll freeze me out. Or he'll tell me it's not me, it's him. Or he'll feel the same way but decide that he needs to marry someone more suitable.'

'Or none of the above. There's no guarantees, Em. It's safer not to try; I agree with you there. But then you'll have to live your whole life wondering what-if. Are you ready to do that?'

She'd thought she was. She'd written the book and bought the T-shirt. But when it came down to the line, all her very valid reasons seemed a lot less valid. 'No,' Emilia said slowly. 'I'm not.'

'If the worst comes to the worst, we're here for you, we're your family, we'll pick you up and heal you. But going through life too scared to put yourself out there isn't living, it's existing, and you deserve more. We all do.'

Emilia turned to her friend, so grateful for her wisdom. All this time she had worried about not being enough, about losing the people she cared about while the women who loved her were supporting her, selflessly making her dreams come true. 'Thank you, Alex. For everything. You, Harriet and Amber are the best family in the world. I am so lucky to have you. I don't know what will happen when I get in there, if things will still be okay with my dad or if I will know what to say to Laurent but, whatever happens, knowing that in two days' time I'll be home with you three makes anything possible.'

Neither Alex or Emilia were the tactile type. Amber was the hugger in their house, Harriet more so since her engagement, but Emilia stepped forward and held her friend close and after one rigid second Alex returned the embrace. Emilia inhaled, drawing courage and strength from the other girl. Alex was right. Emilia had spent her whole life battling with what-ifs. Tonight she was going to lay her ghosts to rest. Tonight she was going to start the rest of her life. She was going to stop being afraid and live.

* * *

The dinner passed with excruciating slowness, Laurent placed between Simone and Bella. He still couldn't read Emilia's stepmother although at times he thought he detected a humour so dry he wasn't sure it was there at all. Bella just wanted to talk puppies and that was a subject he was happy to indulge her in. She was a nice girl, but he realised that she would be bored by the duties an Archduchess needed to take on; like his grandmother, she longed for a simpler life.

But Emilia would handle those duties with aplomb. She was used to being firm and diplomatic, to juggling myriad responsibilities, to long meetings and quick meet and greets. She had everything he needed in an Archduchess.

But even if she hadn't he would want to marry her anyway.

Finally dinner ended and thankfully Laurent escorted the Claytons into the ballroom where the remaining four hundred or so guests waited to greet Mike Clayton and wish him a happy birthday. The room looked magical, like the *Midsummer Night's Dream* Emilia had promised, flowers and fairy lights bedecking every beam and pillar, the guests dressed in a gorgeous display of costumes and gowns.

Laurent took to the stage to welcome everyone officially, to present Mike Clayton with the case of Armarian brandy which was the castle's birthday gift and to remind everyone to be back in the ballroom at midnight for the official birthday cake, and then declared the ball open. Excited chatter broke out as all the guests headed out into the gardens to sample the delights Emilia had planned, or stayed in the ballroom to dance. Although many of the guests had simply added cloaks to cover normal party attire, plenty of others had gone all-out, some in Tudor costumes, others Greek tunics or fairy dress, and some in barely-there strips of glitter or the frock coats and breeches Emilia had threatened him with.

If this had been a traditional ball then Laurent would have been expected to lead the dancing, starting with Simone as wife of the guest of honour, followed by his own mother and then Bella, but the three separate dance areas swept away the usual etiquette and Laurent thankfully slipped away to explore. He had elected to dress simply in his dress uniform. If anyone asked he would claim to be Theseus, the general. All he needed was his Hippolyta. But he snagged a cloak and mask from the table to give himself some privacy, covering his uniform with the cloak and hiding his features with the half-mask.

The disguise was liberating. When he returned to the ballroom it was with complete and rare anonymity; he was free to wander through the ballroom and stand by the French windows, open onto the terrace beyond, without acting either the host or the Prince. In fact, he could go anywhere and nobody would be any the wiser. Now he just needed to find Emilia. He knew she was here somewhere.

Deciding to start in the gardens, he began

to turn, only to come to a stop as a girl entered the room.

She wore a soft yellow dress shot through with silver, the same silver covering half her face, soft brown hair piled high on her head. Hazel eyes searched the room and his pulse began to thrum as they rested on him. He was cloaked and masked, anonymous, but her soft smile recognised and beckoned him. Wordlessly he crossed the room to stand before her.

He bowed with a flourish and she responded with a low gracious curtsey.

'You came?' he said.

'I decided I'm tired of hiding away in the kitchen.' Her gaze swept the room and she sighed in relief. 'It's all going well?'

'Whoever organised it did a brilliant job,' he assured her and was rewarded with another smile.

'It's easy when there is a backdrop like this.'

'How did you recognise me?' he asked.

'I'd know you anywhere.'

At her soft words his pulse sped even more, his blood roaring as it rushed around his body, primal possession seizing him. She knew him and he knew her. She was his as he was hers and nothing could change that. It was wrong to even try.

'I heard you earlier today,' he said quickly, needing her to know before they went any further. 'I heard you with your father, I heard what you said. Thank you. But I didn't need to hear it to know that you are exactly what Armaria needs, because you are what I need.'

'Laurent…'

'I know we haven't known each other long. I know my life is unusual. I know being photographed and speculated about is uncomfortable, but that's not all my life is about. It's about this amazing country and its amazing people. It's about taking chances. There's fun and laughter and love in there, even though I sometimes let duty overwhelm me. I want to share that love and laughter with you. I think I rushed in too quickly before. I don't think you should stay. I think I need to see your life and you need to see mine, that we should date. I think we should get to know each other. I think we should go to the cinema and out for dinner, take long walks and spend slow afternoons just talking, weekends away, maybe a trip to Rome. I'd like to take a Roman holiday with you, scooter and Prosecco and all. I would like to get to know you properly, Emilia. I would like to have the opportunity to woo you.'

'To woo me?' There it was, the dimple at the corner of her mouth, peeping out. He reached out and touched it, relishing the feel of her skin under his.

'To woo you,' he confirmed. 'You see, I already know you're the one for me. I knew it the minute I first saw you, only it took me a while to make sense of what my heart was telling me. But I can see that it might seem a little crazy to you, that you may need some time.'

'Walk with me,' Emilia said. 'I want to see what's outside.'

It wasn't a yes, but nor was it a no and, as

Laurent took the hand she was holding out to him, he felt more full of hope than he had for a long, long time.

She couldn't believe that she was here, walking through the magical light-filled wonderland she had created, listening to the music and the chatter. Actors performed Shakespeare in the rose garden and in the distance, through the trees, acrobats performed a gravity-defying set. To her right, on an outdoor stage, two dancers performed a *pas de deux* of such breathtaking beauty all she could do was stand and stare until the last lift. In the marquee ahead of them partygoers danced to the rock her father adored, in the ballroom behind her couples were sweeping around the floor in a traditional waltz. People walked by, holding a whole variety of drinks or foods, their costumes bright and ornate.

And as she walked and stood and marvelled there was Laurent, solid and real, his hand in hers. The cloak hid his uniform, the mask half his face, but she'd know that mouth anywhere, the blue eyes, the way he held his body. The way he looked at her as if he saw her soul.

Happiness rippled through her, so rare and fragile but real. It had been so long since she had felt this way and it was down to the man next to her. The way he made her feel, the way he felt about her. 'You talked to Dad about me?'

She felt him tense and squeezed his hand reassuringly.

'A little, the first day they arrived.'

'I don't know what you said but he said you didn't mince your words. You didn't need to do that for me, Laurent—what about the factory?'

'The factory is important, you know that. But integrity is important too. What kind of man would I be to sell out love for profit?'

Love. Emilia took a deep breath. It was time she dared to show her feelings, time to dare to be vulnerable. 'You told me once that duty dictated who you are and what you did.

But it doesn't. You just know what's right. It's part of you, innate. But me? Fear has dictated everything for me. Fear of not being enough, fear of being left.'

'That's understandable. Your experiences would make anyone feel that way.'

'I told you I couldn't be with you and I meant it. I thought that the memories of one night would be the most I would ever get. That a lifetime with someone is too scary to dream of, too out of reach. Better to flame briefly and brightly and die than burn out.'

His clasp tightened and he turned to face her, tilting her chin so she met his fearless gaze. Emilia's stomach tightened as she saw the heat in the depths of his eyes, a heat her whole body yearned to match. 'You told me to go and, like a fool, I listened. But I've changed my mind. I'm not going anywhere. A flame doesn't have to burn out; it can be constant. You light up my life, Emilia Clayton. I want to learn to read your every thought and fleeting look. I want shared jokes and known danger areas. I want to see you first thing in the morning and last thing at night. And I'll be dammed if I spend the rest of my life thinking *What-if?* because I *know*. I shouldn't know because I'm a rational man and I don't believe in love at first sight, but I *know* we'll be happy. If I was writing that film of yours then your Princess and Cary Grant...'

'Gregory Peck.'

He squeezed her hand. 'Your Princess and Gregory Peck get on that scooter and they ride off into the sunset together. I want to ride into every sunset with you. I am not going to leave you.'

'I wanted you to,' she confessed. 'Because that was easier than actually trying and it not working out. Of really getting to know you and care for you and then you leaving. That scared me—scares me—most of all. You can't promise that won't happen—no one can.'

'Are you saying you don't want to try?'

'No. At least, a bit of me is still yelling loudly that this is too much of a risk, that it's better to walk away now. But I am sick of being afraid, tired of letting what happened in the past define me. I don't want to look back at a life half lived, half loved. I want to look back at a life where I gave it my all.'

'And is there space in that life for me?'

Emilia took a deep breath. 'It seems so absurd after so short a time, but I can't imagine my life without you in it. I don't want to imagine my life without you in it. So if you want to be there, then yes, there's space.' She trembled as she said the words, at how vulnerable she was making herself, knowing that now they were said there was no unsaying them, now she was allowing herself to really feel there was no way of guarding her heart. 'There's space to learn each other's worlds. For films and walks on the beach, for dinners and brunches. For all the in-betweens.'

'I want to be there. I know it won't be easy. You live in England, I here, we both have lives and duties. But I promised to woo you, Emilia, and that's exactly what I intend to do.'

'I like a man who keeps his promises,' she whispered as his mouth found hers. The ball, her fears, her responsibilities all disappeared under his embrace. She pulled back, cupping his face in hers. 'I don't need wooing, Laurent. I'm in. I'm yours if you're sure.'

'I'm sure,' he vowed. 'I know where the end point is. I know that in six months, or a year, one day I'll know the time is right, that you'll be ready and I'll ask you to be my Archduchess and you'll make the most splendid Archduchess Armaria has ever known. But, more importantly, I'll ask you to be my wife. Not just because you're suitable, but because I love you and I can't imagine a life that doesn't have you in it.'

'Keep remembering those words,' Emilia said, eyes burning with unshed tears—but, for the first time she could remember they were tears of happiness. 'They'll be perfect for the proposal.'

'Come on.' Laurent started to walk and Emilia allowed him to pull her along.

'Where are we going?'

'I want to dance with my beautiful duchess-to-be. In front of everyone.'

They'd reached the ballroom. Emilia could see her dad twirling Simone around. He looked so happy, Simone smiling up at him. She might not like the way they'd found each other but she couldn't deny they suited each other. In the opposite corner Bella was dancing with Laurent's second cousin, her face lit up. Laurent halted and then slowly, deliberately removed his gown and mask before taking Emilia's mask off her. She shivered as his fingers brushed her cheek.

'No more hiding,' he told her. 'From now on we're a team—and we face all our fears together.'

Emilia could barely speak. She was no longer alone. This glorious, strong man needed her—and she needed him. 'Together,' she repeated. 'I'll do my best to make sure we both live happily ever after.'

'In that case—' he bowed '—will you do me the honour?' Laurent held out his hand and she took it.

'Always,' she promised.

His eyes flared and as he swept her into the dance his mouth found hers. Emilia kissed him back with all the intensity and passion and love she had, not caring who was watching. No more being afraid. No more watching from the sidelines. With Laurent by her side she could face and be anything. With Laurent she was finally free.

She broke the kiss and cupped his face in her hands. 'I love you,' she said. 'Not because you're an Archduke and a prince, not because you're the best person I have ever met, not because you make me feel invincible. I love you because you have the biggest heart, because you make me laugh, because you knew me the moment we met and I knew you too. I love you because the thought of spending my life with you makes me impatient to get started. I love you because you're you.'

Laurent smiled down, infinitely tender, infinitely dear. 'I love you, Emilia Clayton,' he said. And as the music swelled and he twirled her back into the waltz Emilia knew she would never be alone again.

* * * * *

LET'S TALK
Romance

For exclusive extracts, competitions
and special offers, find us online:

01   502   50   504   5

517   518